SNOWBIRD
WINTER

Also by Sue Welford

Ghost in the Mirror

SNOWBIRD
WINTER
Sue Welford

MAMMOTH

First published in Great Britain 1994
by Oxford University Press
Published 1995 by Mammoth
an imprint of Reed International Books Ltd
Michelin House, 81 Fulham Road, London SW3 6RB
and Auckland, Melbourne, Singapore and Toronto

Text copyright © Sue Welford 1994

The right of Sue Welford to be identified as author of this
work has been asserted by her in accordance with
the Copyright, Designs and Patents Act 1988

ISBN 0 7497 1881 1

Printed and bound in Great Britain
by Cox & Wyman Ltd, Reading, Berkshire

For
Bebe Lou
and
Boy
With Love

JOURNAL OF EXPLORER SHIP ICE VOYAGER — ZD 6874210.
CREWMASTER'S ENTRY

After being attacked by alien warships we have suffered
space/time displacement due to the malfunction of our
continuum converter. Whilst undergoing repairs we have
drifted into an uncharted galaxy approximately five hundred
thousand million light watches from home.

During the attack two members of our crew have been injured,
one fatally. Scanner readouts show suspended life-signs. In
accordance with crewmember Shannah's wishes a suitably
climatic world will be found to rest before her last flight.

A world for the resting of crewmember Shannah has been
located. A dispensing party was dispatched at first watch. The
small planet appears to have compatibility of climate and
terrain with Shannah's homebase. Locators report body
entombed in area of snowbound flatlands of a tiny planet-island
in the northern hemisphere. The country was covered by
darkness and no encounters with aliens took place.
Crewtechnicians report continuum converter due to refunction
three watches from 6874211.

1

Brin—The Legacy

'Who's Aunt Winnie?'

'Shh!' Brin frowned at her sister Toni and held her finger to her lips. From her parents' study came the sound of murmuring voices. 'I'm trying to hear what they say,' she hissed.

'Well, who *is* she?'

'Who *was* she you mean. She's dead.'

'Well all right then, Brin, who *was* she.'

'She was Dad's old aunt—great-aunt, I think. One he didn't know he had.'

'Yeah, I bet.'

'Honestly. I heard Dad talking on the phone.'

'Does great mean she was fat?'

'Don't be stupid, Toni. For a ten year old you can be really thick sometimes. Even Tom knows what a great-aunt is. Don't you, Tom?'

Thomas, their six-year-old hyperactive brother, lay on the floor staring at the television screen even though it was switched off.

'Yep.' Thomas rolled over on his back. 'Why can't we have telly on?' He got up and wrenched one of the Indian shawls off the sofa. He began charging around the room with it round his shoulders singing 'Batman'.

'Ssh, Tom! Mum and Dad are talking to someone important. A solicitor. And I'm trying to hear what they're saying!'

Thomas plonked himself down on the settee. He sighed and began sucking his thumb. 'I'm bored,' he moaned.

Brin gave up trying to listen through the wall. She moved aside a pile of magazines, knelt up on the window seat and looked out. The sun was setting over St Paul's cathedral. The dome looked as if it was on fire. In the courtyard below,

1

pigeons pecked. The scarlet geraniums that once looked like summer splashes of blood were dry and faded. Someone had swept the beer cans thrown over the wall into a pile in the corner. Brin leaned her cheek against the cool pane of glass. The roar of traffic was like thunder. She closed her eyes and tried to imagine she was on that flower-strewn desert island she'd seen on a video at school that day.

'What's a . . . a hotchpotch, Brin?' Toni was trying to learn her spellings. She'd been chewing her pen and had a blue mouth.

Brin opened her eyes. 'It's a whole mixture of different things, colours, people . . .'

'What, like us?'

Brin smiled. When Toni wasn't being horrible she could be quite sweet. 'Yes, Toni,' she said, 'a bit like us.'

Brin supposed her family was a bit of a hotchpotch. Their mother, Alex, was a teacher. David, their father, did something with computers. Brin wasn't quite sure what. Then there was her, and Toni, and Thomas. The three children weren't at all alike. Brin was the dreamy type. She read a lot and collected things. Toni liked boys and playing football. And Tom . . . well, Tom liked anything to do with Thunderbirds and chocolate and hated anything to do with going to bed. Then there was Zhivago, their hamster. He was Russian. The family had a couple of pet spiders, too. There was Germaine who lived in a corner of the bathroom ceiling. Sometimes she fell into the basin and had to be rescued. The other spider was called Emily after some suffragette person. Brin wasn't quite sure who. Brin suddenly realized she hadn't seen Emily for ages. She used to live in the central heating grille in the front room.

The flat was a bit of a hotchpotch, too. There were lots of things Alex and David had brought back from their trip to India. That was before any of the children were born. The photograph on the bookshelves showed them standing in front of the Taj Mahal. They were wearing the most terrible flared denims, cotton shirts, and what Brin thought were yukky platform shoes. Her dad had got long hair and sideburns and her mum's hair was permed all over in a wild frizz. Brin really didn't know why they kept the photo out for everyone to see. She hid it when her friends came.

Tom was just about to start using the settee as a trampoline when their parents and the important visitor came out of the study. They shook hands. Brin's father went with her to the door.

'Thanks for bringing the forms for us to sign, Ms Taylor. And for telling us about my aunt. Shall I come down in the lift with you?'

The important visitor shook her head. 'No, I'll be fine. Bye, children.'

'Bye,' they chorused although they didn't even know her. Brin didn't much like being included in the 'children' bit. At thirteen she considered herself past that stage.

Brin's father went into the kitchen. When he came back, Alex said, 'Family conference.'

Tom groaned. 'I've missed *Quick Draw McGraw*.'

David put down the tray of crisps and fizzy drinks he'd brought in from the kitchen. He picked Tom up, hoisting him on to his shoulder as if he was a sack of onions. His head almost hit the light.

'Careful, David,' their mother smiled.

The children sat on the sofa, munching crisps and swigging cans of Coke. Tom wasn't allowed Coke because he was allergic to the artificial colourings. He wasn't really allowed crisps, either, but seemed to be getting away with it this time. Brin thought it must be pretty rotten having to have an apple while other people were scoffing crisps. Their father sat on the floor, cross-legged. His jeans were split at the knee.

The children looked at their parents expectantly. Sometimes family conferences were serious. They must read more books and watch less TV. They must try harder at school. They must stop leaving lights on all over the place. The family weren't going away for a holiday that year but would have days out. They knew that meant the British Museum and the Victoria and Albert, to name only two. They always groaned. It didn't make any difference. They went anyway. By the time Brin was ten she knew them both inside out . . . and the National Gallery.

Sometimes though, family conferences were exciting. Like the time their mother told them she was going to have another baby. Then there was the sad one when their father told them she'd had a miscarriage. There wasn't going to be a baby after all. They'd all felt miserable that day, even Tom who'd only been four at the time.

This particular conference didn't turn out to be serious or sad or exciting. In fact it turned out to be a hotchpotch of all three.

And what came after turned out to be mysterious and very scary, although Brin didn't realize it at the time.

2

Chris—'Dimmocks'

Chris sat at the kitchen table trying to concentrate on his homework. It was no good, he'd never get the hang of Shakespeare if he lived to be a hundred.

'I wonder what'll happen to the house now the old girl's gone, John?'

Mrs Carter put powder into the dishwasher and slammed the door. Her husband, reading *Farmers and Growers* at the kitchen table, looked up.

'I don't know. State the place is in, it should be pulled down.'

'It's not that bad, is it?' Chris looked at his father.

'How long since you been inside it, boy?'

Chris shrugged. He flicked back the lock of shaggy brown hair that had fallen over his eyes. 'Dunno . . . er, in the summer I suppose. When I took in those sweet peas Mum asked me to pick.'

'It was so strange,' Chris's mother said. 'Winnie knew it was her birthday but couldn't remember how old she was.'

'She must have been over ninety,' Mr Carter said. 'Ben Smith's mother-in-law knew her when she was a young girl. *She* was over seventy when she died and that was years ago . . .'

'Yes, poor old Winnie. She had a job remembering her name sometimes, but she told me about her fifteenth birthday party as if it was yesterday.'

Chris chewed the end of his Biro. 'July, wasn't it? I'd just broken up for the holidays when I took her those flowers.'

Mrs Carter sighed. 'Yes, I'm afraid she really went downhill after that.'

Chris's father snorted. 'Come off it, Anne, the old girl had been a bit batty as long as I can remember.'

5

kind, John. She wasn't batty, she was just lonely
. and very old.'

why she did all those weird things?' Chris asked.

, I'm afraid it was.'

'. . . walking along the river at night, talking to herself.
You know I'm really surprised she didn't fall in and drown.'

'Me too.' Mrs Carter shivered. 'Hope to God I never get like
that.'

'We'd have you put down.' Chris's father laughed.

'When did her husband die, Mum?'

'Oh, years and years ago, before we moved here. There
weren't any children.'

'Poor old thing.'

'Yes. I wish I could have done more for her.'

'What? You did more than anyone else,' Mr Carter said. 'If
it hadn't been for you, Anne, she might have lain at the
bottom of those stairs for weeks before anyone discovered
her. God knows what she was doing in that old tower
anyway. The place is falling to bits . . .'

'Yes, but she still died, didn't she?' Mrs Carter's voice was
sad, full of regret. 'When I did eventually find her, it was too
late. She'd already developed pneumonia.'

'Well, at least her last few days in hospital were spent in
comfort. It's better to die in a hospital bed than on a cold
wooden floor.'

'Yes,' Mrs Carter sighed. 'I suppose you're right, John.' She
looked thoughtful. 'You know, I wish I knew what happened
to that necklace.'

'What necklace, Mum?' It was the first time Chris had
heard about any necklace.

'That locket she always wore. Don't say you'd never
noticed?'

Chris shrugged. He couldn't ever remember old Mrs
Mirston wearing anything but holey old jumpers and
trousers that looked as if they'd come from a jumble sale. Let
alone jewellery. 'Don't know what you're talking about,' he
said.

6

'Your mum means that gold locket she always wore underneath her woollies—' Chris's father said.

'Yes . . . ' Mrs Carter interrupted. 'It was the only piece of jewellery she had left.'

'What happened to the rest of it?'

'She'd sold everything else to pay the bills. She definitely had the locket on the day before I found her. I remember remarking on it. Lovely thing it was. Antique. I told the solicitor about it when she took away all those documents to look at. I wouldn't have wanted her to think I'd taken anything.'

'What did the solicitor say?'

'She said not to worry. It would probably turn up. Maybe Winnie put it somewhere and had forgotten where. She certainly didn't have it on when she fell down those stairs.' Mrs Carter's voice was full of sorrow. 'I was really fond of her, you know.' She sniffed.

Chris felt sad too, talking about Mrs Mirston. She'd been a nice old thing, even though she was a bit weird. He'd run errands for her when he was a kid. Used to take her dog out until it died of old age. Chris had fed the rabbits, helped her with the garden sometimes. There was nothing she didn't know about wildlife and plants and things. He remembered one summer he had even taken her out in his boat. She'd worn a long dress and a floppy straw hat. The dress had been creased, marked with brown stains. It had obviously been folded away for years. It was a long time, she said, since a young man had taken her rowing. Chris remembered she was full of Fenland tales; river fairs at Cambridge, skating matches when the meres and rivers were frozen solid. 'People used to compete for prizes of bread and meat they were so poor,' she'd said. That was before she seemed to forget completely who Chris was and shouted at him for trespassing when he rowed past the old boathouse at the end of her garden. He'd been quite upset at the time.

'Didn't she have any relatives at all then?' Chris put down his book.

'A nephew apparently . . .' Mrs Carter said, '. . . in London. That solicitor who came to look at the house told me he answered an advertisement in the paper . . . you know, asking if anyone was related to Winnie Mirston. You see them in the *Evening News* sometimes.'

'Didn't the nephew know about her before then?' Chris asked.

'I suppose not. I used to ask her about her family but she said she lost touch with them all years ago. They didn't approve of her marrying an artist apparently.'

'Why on earth not?'

'I don't know. I suppose it wasn't respectable in those days.'

Chris couldn't imagine why being an artist wasn't respectable.

'I suppose the house will go to the nephew, then?' Mr Carter got up. He went into the lobby to put his boots on. 'Good luck, that's what I say. I wouldn't want to be saddled with a place like that. Been neglected all this time. Maybe they'll pull it down and build a modern bungalow.'

Mrs Carter made a face. 'Good God, I hope not.'

'Where you going, Dad?' Chris asked.

'Just to lock the barn. It doesn't look as if that lorry's coming with the fertilizer until tomorrow. Then I think I'll take a stroll along the river.'

'Hang on, I'll come with you.' Chris closed his English file with a bang and put away his pen.

'You finished your homework?'

'Yes, Mum . . . honestly.'

Outside, the sun was setting over the Fen. Chris could smell the dark, acidic smell of the peat. High up, a V-shaped formation of wild geese flew across the red-edged sky. They were arriving early this year. Sign of a hard, Fenland winter old Ben Smith, the reedcutter, would say. Like the ones Winnie remembered, maybe? A mist was already rising ghost-grey from the marshes. The sharp tang of autumn hung in the air. Chris zipped up his anorak and ran after his father.

'I wonder if anyone'll move in then?' he said, trying to match his father's long strides.

'Where?' Chris's father whistled to Wag, the spaniel, who had already gone off hunting for something in the reeds.

'Dimmocks.'

'Dunno, son.'

It would seem weird, someone else living in the old place.

Mr Carter raised his eyebrows. 'This nephew could have a family, I suppose.'

'What, you mean . . . kids?'

'Why not?'

'Oh, no . . .'

John Carter laughed. 'Don't you fancy having other children around then, boy?'

'No, I do not,' Chris said vehemently.

'You won't have any choice, I'm afraid.'

Chris looked glum. His father grinned and put his arm across Chris's shoulders. 'Don't worry, son. Whoever it is I don't suppose they'll bother us.'

'No.'

In spite of his father's words, Chris felt apprehensive. He was used to being on his own. No brothers or sisters. No one his own age living within miles of the farm. Living out in the wild, flat Fenlands. Everyone at school thought *he* was a bit of a hermit, never mind old Winnie. It wasn't that. He just liked his own company. The last thing he wanted was a load of townies living close by. Dropping litter and stuff . . . frightening the wildlife. What on earth could kids brought up in a city know about the countryside? He hated the very thought of it.

For some strange reason he couldn't fathom, Chris suddenly thought of that huge bird he'd seen last year. He'd never seen anything like it before. It definitely had not been a swan, its neck was far too short. Then he'd thought it might

9

be a goose, although it had been too far away to really tell *what* kind of bird it was. Sometimes flocks of pink-footed geese from North America or dark-breasted brent geese from the Arctic would have an odd member of another species amongst them. He had wondered if it might be a snow-goose although, as far as he knew, one had never been seen in this part of the world. Chris knew they sometimes spent a vagrant winter down the west coast of Britain. He supposed one could have escaped from a wildfowl collection some-where and ended up in the Fens but it wasn't very likely.

Chris had seen the strange bird on one of those grey evenings when the low-lying river mist made everything look like a distortion of reality. You never really could tell what you were seeing on an evening like that. Even an ordinary old cow looked like some hazy creature from another world if it loomed up out of the mist in front of you. Whatever this bird had been, it was huge and white and it had made no sound at all. Even at that distance, the honking of geese could be heard for miles across the wide, fenland sky. Chris hadn't thought about it for ages. What if it came back this year and the new people scared it off? Be just his luck.

Chris and his father were passing Mrs Mirston's house. Chris suddenly felt an overwhelming curiosity to look inside. To see if it was changed now the old girl was dead.

'Dad, I'm just going to look.'

'What at?'

'The house.'

'Don't you go trespassing, boy. Just because it's empty doesn't mean any Tom, Dick, or Harry can go exploring the place.'

'I won't. I'm only going to look.'

Chris wished his parents would stop calling him 'boy'. He wasn't a kid any more.

Dimmocks stood silent in the darkening twilight. Chris leaned his elbows on the gate and stared at the neglected garden. A web of undergrowth covered what was once a rockery. Up one wall of the house, the flower heads of an unruly clematis had turned into a tangle of old man's beard. It covered two of the upstairs windows like a grey fog. The other two, and the attic windows above, were spangled gold in the setting sun. Between the criss-cross brown oak beams the plaster was cracked and flaking. Tiles were missing off the front porch. A regiment of unwashed milk bottles guarded the step.

Chris shivered. There was something really creepy about Dimmocks. There always had been. Maybe it was the old mill-tower attached to the end? That looked even more mysterious than usual in the twilight. Chris used to make up ghost stories about it when he was small. He still had them somewhere, written in an old shorthand note-pad his aunty had given him. It was stuffed in the back of his bedroom cupboard behind his Star Wars toys and other childish things he'd long since given up. He had written the stories when he was going through his vampire stage. He'd shown them to his mother. She'd laughed, said Chris had a terrific imagination but might be better concentrating on his maths.

Chris grinned to himself. The tower looked just the right place to harbour bats. It was poor old Winnie who'd been bats. Chris remembered her stomping along the lane in her wellies and tatty old coat. Pushing that big old pram that looked like it was the first one ever invented. She carried wood in it for the fire. Or groceries in the days when the mobile shop still stopped on the corner.

Chris pushed open the gate and walked up the path. Weeds grew between the bricks beneath his feet. He cupped his hands round his eyes and put his face to the window. The place wasn't empty at all. Mrs Mirston's stuff was still in there. He could see an old red settee by the fireplace. An armchair in the corner. On the wall opposite the window something moved. A face? A pale figure? Chris jumped back. Then he laughed out loud. It was only his own reflection in a mirror. Nevertheless, he shivered. It had given him quite a scare. The chill of the evening seemed to have got right inside his bones.

Chris turned and went back through the gate. He shut it behind him. He took one more look at the house. His father was right. Whoever inherited the place had a job on their hands that was for sure.

' Vampires and all.

3

Brin—The Old Mill Tower

'. . . and so we'll be moving after half term.'

Toni burst into tears as her father spoke.

Alex hugged her. 'Come on, Ant (it was her pet name . . . Antonia . . . Ant . . .) it won't be so bad. They might even let you play in the football team at school.'

Toni stamped her foot. She pushed her mother away. 'No they won't. They never do. And I'll have to leave all my friends. I don't want to move to a crummy old house in the middle of nowhere. My friend Justin's been there on a boat and says it's flat and boring. No buildings or anything hardly. Just horrible black soil and rivers.' She picked up a cushion and threw it across the room. Her face was red, tear stained. 'You lot can go . . . I'm staying in London, so there.' Wailing, she ran upstairs. Her bedroom door slammed.

Alex winced. 'That's woken Tom, I bet.' They listened for a minute, breaths held. When Tom went to bed at a civilized hour, the family celebrated . . . quietly.

When they had decided hell wasn't going to be let loose, Brin's parents looked at her.

'Well, Brin . . . ?' David said. He raised his eyebrows.

Brin shrugged. 'I'll hate changing schools, of course, but . . .'

'Darling, there's some really good schools in Cambridge . . . I know you'll have to leave all your friends, but it's an opportunity of a lifetime, don't you see? You know we've always wanted to get out of the city, bring you kids up in the country. We'd like to grow our own vegetables. Get away from all the pollution . . .'

Brin smiled at her mother. She was trying so hard to convince Brin of all the things she already knew. 'It's OK, Mum . . . Dad . . . er . . . will Emma be able to come and stay?'

13

Brin felt if she could have her friends to stay it wouldn't be so bad.

Her father put his arm round her. 'Of course she will, Brin. The house isn't huge but I'm sure we'll find room. Anyone you like can come and stay.'

'When are we going to see it?'

'This weekend.'

'What about your job, Mum. And Dad's?'

Alex and David exchanged glances.

'Well,' David said, 'Alex is going to carry on teaching, coming up by train every day and I'm going to work from home and look after you lot.'

'Will we be able to swim in the river?' Tom appeared at the top of the stairs. He looked totally refreshed from his half hour's sleep. He climbed on to the bannisters and sat there waving his legs around. Brin heard her mother sigh.

'We'll be able to do anything we like, Tom,' David said. 'All that fenland air might make him sleep,' he added under his breath.

Tom's eyes were wide. 'Will I be able to take my Thunderbirds?'

David laughed. 'Of course you will. We'll take everything with us . . . all your toys . . . everything.'

'Wow!' Tom climbed off the bannisters. He ran downstairs. Then he ran up again waving his arms. His Thunderbird figures had appeared miraculously from his pyjama trousers. 'F.A.B.,' he shouted before disappearing into his room. They heard him running round then he came out and ran back down the stairs.

'What about Toni?' Brin asked.

'Come on, Brin. You know Toni. She has to make a fuss, it's against her principles not to.' Alex got up.

Brin smiled. Mum was right. As usual.

'OK, Thomas,' Alex said. 'BED!'

'But, Mum . . .' Brin heard him say as his mother took hold of his arm and propelled him upstairs. 'Bed's boring . . .'

* * *

They had to collect the key from the people who lived along the lane. Highfen Farm it said on the gate although Brin couldn't see any cows or sheep. There were chickens pecking about in the field. A notice said 'Free Range Eggs'. A dog barked somewhere from the back. Dark machines crouched like monsters in a huge barn. A mountain of wooden boxes ran the whole length of the wall.

No one answered the bell.

'Go round the back, see if there's anyone about,' David called from the car.

Round the back, a boat was propped up against the side of a shed. Under a tree, a brown and white spaniel in a pen stood up with its front paws on the wire. It barked furiously. On the lawn a brightly coloured duck in a cage pecked at a plastic bowl full of water. As Brin bent down to look she could see it had something wrong with its leg. She put her finger through the wire. The duck pecked at it.

'I suppose you thought it was a worm,' Brin said, waggling her finger. She wished she could stroke its shiny feathers. They looked so soft and beautiful.

When Brin stood up there was a boy standing in the doorway of the shed. He had a paint brush in his hand. He had hair that looked as if it had been cut with a bread knife. A bit stuck up on the crown of his head as if he had lain on it all wrong. He looked surprised to see her.

Brin smiled. 'Hi.'

'Hello,' he said, going a bit red.

'Is this your duck?'

'No, it's a wild one, its leg was injured.'

'What happened to it?'

'Got tangled in some nylon fishing line, cut it badly.'

'Poor thing,' Brin bent down again but the duck limped away into its little house.

'Do you like birds?' the boy asked.

Brin shrugged. 'Yes . . . I suppose so. But in London all we see are millions of pigeons and sparrows and messy old starlings.'

The boy looked surprised. As if he thought the country was the only place allowed to have more than one kind of bird.

'There's loads of different species around here,' he said. 'Ducks, grebes, herons . . . geese come in winter. Warblers, moorhens . . . swans,' he added like an afterthought. 'You name it . . .'

'We have swans on the Thames. And ducks. I forgot about them.'

'Oh, yeah?' He raised his eyebrows.

Brin thought it was about time she told the boy who she was. 'We've come for the key,' she explained.

He looked blank. 'Key . . .?'

'To . . . er . . . Dimmocks. My aunt's old house.'

The boy's face cleared. 'Oh, you must be . . . I thought you'd come for some eggs. Hang on, I'll get it.' He went into the house. Brin followed but waited outside the back door. Even from there she could smell something cooking. It made her mouth water. 'My mum and dad've gone to Ely shopping,' the boy called from inside. 'Mum said you would probably come this morning.' He came back out. 'Good excuse for me not to go with them.' He grinned then went red again.

'Yes.' Brin knew exactly what he meant. Shopping with parents, fathers especially, was pure hell.

The boy handed her a jangle of keys. 'Mrs Mirston was your aunt then?'

'My great-great-aunt,' Brin said. 'Although I never met her. Did you know her?'

'Yes.'

'Was she nice?'

The boy hesitated. 'Er . . . yeah, she was OK.'

He didn't look too sure. The dog was still barking and scrabbling frantically at the door of his pen.

'What's your dog's name?' Brin asked.

'Wag . . .'

'My dad says we might be able to have a dog when we come to live here. We've never been able to before, living in a flat and all . . .'

'Old Ben . . . he's going to let his bitch have puppies.'

'Who's Ben?'

'He works for the River Authority. He's a reedcutter.'

'Oh . . .'

'I could ask him if you like . . . about a puppy?'

'I'd better ask Dad first . . . you know . . . him saying we could have a dog might have been a bribe . . . you know what parents are like. They don't always mean what they say.'

Brin's father was really quite good at meaning what he said but Brin felt you could never be quite sure.

'Yes . . . OK.' The boy looked away. Brin could see he'd gone red again.

She waved the keys. 'Thanks for these.'

'OK . . . er . . .'

Brin waited.

'Er . . . are you going to live there then . . . er . . . Dimmocks, I mean?'

'Yes.'

The boy lowered his eyes. 'Oh.'

Brin didn't think he looked very pleased at the prospect.

The boy came round to the front of the house with her. He stood, watching the car drive away. His wellies looked about four sizes too big. Brin thought they were probably his dad's.

'Well, what was his name?' Alex asked.

'Whose name?' Toni piped up from the depths of the back seat.

'The boy,' Alex said.

Toni sat up sharply. 'What boy?' Her cycling helmet almost banged the roof.

'You'd have seen him if you weren't sulking.'

'Well . . . did you ask him?' Alex said. She leaned forward and turned off her Beatles tape. Much to everyone's relief.

'No, Mum,' Brin said.

'Well, that wasn't very friendly. If we're going to be neighbours . . .'

'Mum, I don't go round asking strange boys their names.'

'Why not?' asked Tom, poking Brin with his Thunderbird 3.

17

'I just don't that's all.' She pushed him away. Two hours in the back of a car with Tom was enough to try anyone's patience. 'For God's sake, Tom . . .!'

'I would have done,' Toni said. 'How old was he?'

'How do I know? God, Toni, I'm not a detective.'

'Now, now, you kids,' their father said.

'Well, how old do you *think* he was?' Toni asked.

'About a hundred and eight I should think,' Brin said irritably.

'Too old for you, Toni,' their father grinned at them in the mirror.

'Ha ha.' Toni's face dropped into sulking mode again.

Toni was still snotty when they got to the house. She even refused to get out of the car so they just left her there.

'Her curiosity will get the better of her, don't worry,' their mother said. 'She'll soon come round when she gets hungry.'

Brin stayed in the garden. She wanted to look at the house from the outside first. Brin often thought houses were like people. Even if the outside was really ugly, the inside might be beautiful. And the other way round. This house wasn't exactly ugly. Or exactly beautiful. It was just different from anything else Brin had ever seen. Even in the British Museum.

The pinkish plaster was cracked and peeling. It looked damp, as if water from the river had seeped into the foundations. The windows were like eyes, staring, trying to work out what kind of person Brin was. Trying to decide if it would like her living there. Just as she was trying to work out what kind of house it was and how she would like having to live there for the next, goodness knows how many, years. Maybe even the whole of the rest of her life.

Built on to the far end was a sort of squarish wooden tower. It was neglected, more fallen into decay than the rest of the house. It looked as if it had once been painted white. Creeping fingers of ivy grew up the side, clinging on to the cladding for dear life. Brin's father had said it had been a windmill, used to pump water from the surrounding land into the river. The sails had long since been removed.

Brin went to one of the cottage windows and peered inside. She could hear her parents moving about. She could hear her mother calling something to her father. Tom was running up and down the stairs. Probably waving Scott Tracy around pretending he was off on some mission with International Rescue. On the wall opposite the window, a mirror showed a misty reflection of a face peeping in like an intruder. Pale hair tied on top, dangly ear-rings Brin had borrowed from her mum. She rubbed the dirty glass with her finger and the image became clearer. Then Tom's face appeared, green baseball cap skew-whiff on his head. He stuck his tongue out then squashed his nose against the other side of the pane.

'Come in, Brin,' he shouted. 'It's like a castle in here.'

Brin heard a voice at her elbow. 'I'm not going in there, filthy old place . . .'

She turned and put her arm round her sister. 'Come on, Ant, don't be a pain.'

Toni wrenched off her cycling helmet. Her eyes filled with tears. 'I don't *want* to live in this boring flat old place.' She shuddered. 'And the house looks . . .'

'What?'

'It looks cold. A winter house.'

'Toni, you're just being daft.'

But, in spite of her words, Brin knew exactly what she meant.

'Aren't you coming in, you two?' Alex appeared at the front door.

Toni looked down at the ground.

'Go on.' Brin gave her a slight shove. Toni tried to punch her but she dodged. 'I'll be in in a minute,' she said.

She wanted to see the inside of the tower first.

'Where you going?' her mother asked, frowning.

'I'm just going to have a look at the tower.'

'Well, be careful. David said it was a bit rickety.'

The door wasn't locked. As Brin pushed it open, a shower of dust and cobwebs fell on to her head. She brushed them

19

away and looked up. In front of her was a steep wooden staircase. Its narrow treads were warped and worn. At the top she could see a square hatchway cut out of the wooden ceiling. Light shone down through the dust like a motorway to heaven. Brin stepped over the threshold. She took a deep breath. And sneezed. Above, there was a rustling, a swishing noise as if a great bird had been disturbed by the noise. Then everything went quiet. Brin guessed it must be pigeons. They always like nesting in towers.

From somewhere outside, Brin heard her father call. Then Tom's high voice. She ignored them. She had the oddest feeling that if she didn't explore the tower now, that minute, she might miss something.

Holding on to the shaky bannister, Brin climbed carefully up. Below, the ground floor of the old mill-tower was strewn with rubbish. Smelly old newspapers. Wooden boxes. Flower pots. A rusty old pram, piled high with old sacks, that looked as if it was falling to bits. One corner was full of autumn leaves pushed under the door by the fierce fenland blows. Brin shivered. Alex had bought a book about the Cambridgeshire Fens. She was keen on that kind of thing. Reading up about places before you visited them. Or, in this case, went to live in them. There were more guide books in the sideboard drawer than most people have knives and forks. Brin hadn't got round to reading the Cambridgeshire book but her mother said it was full of folk tales. Dead moons, witches, and giants. Mysterious black dogs and people getting lost in the snow. Half-way up those rickety stairs in that creepy old mill-tower, it wasn't hard to imagine how tales like that had grown up over the years. Perhaps Toni was right about coming to live here? Maybe it *would* be a mistake?

Something, though, made Brin go on to the top. Curiosity, she supposed. And the belief that once you'd started something, you'd flipping well got to finish it.

She stepped through the hole and stood up straight. In the wall opposite was a window. Brin walked cautiously towards it, testing each wooden floorboard as she went. They creaked and squeaked beneath her weight. As she reached the window and looked out Brin knew what had made her go up there. The view from the top of the mill-tower was totally brilliant. Looking out through the broken glass, Brin felt she was the only person in the universe. In front of her stretched endless miles of black and green Fenland. The shining ribbons of the river and its adjoining lodes cut the land into sections. The black, ploughed ridges of the fields had been drawn by a giant's hand. In the breeze, sedges waved in time to some silent music and way above the trees a great flock of dark birds were tiny witches milling about in the sky. In the far distance, almost invisible to the naked eye, a small cluster of doll houses made hardly a bump in the landscape. Along by the bridge the reflections of the motor cruisers looked like Siamese twins. If Brin craned her neck she could see the island of Ely and its cathedral boiling up from the flatlands like a fairy castle. Her father had said you could see it from almost anywhere in the Fens.

Then Brin noticed a family of six or seven swans gliding along the river towards the house. Two were white, the rest a murky grey. As she watched, they swam silently past without giving the house a glance. Their heads were proud, held high. It was almost as if the house, the mill-tower, weren't there at all. As if the river was their domain and anything, any signs of human habitation were only there to be ignored.

Brin took a deep breath. She could smell fresh air. Water. She could even smell the wind that touched her face as it passed. She closed her eyes and could still see the landscape as if it had been etched on her brain for ever. She remembered someone had told Toni the land was flat and boring. But Brin found herself loving the flatness. Somehow it put the sky into perspective.

Downstairs, she heard a voice. 'Brin, you up there?'

'Yes, Dad.' Brin went to the top of the stairs.

'Is it safe?'

'It's a bit wobbly. Come up though, the view's brilliant.'

'Wow!' David said when he got to the window. 'Wow . . .' He just stood and stared for a minute. Then he turned. 'Do you think you're going to like living here, Brinna?'

'Yes.' Brin said it straight away. Without even thinking.

David pulled up a wooden box. He brushed the dirt off. He patted it. 'Hey, come and sit with me a minute.'

'What's all this stuff?' Brin looked around the room. Amidst the mess of ruined birds' nests, twigs, leaves, and rubbish were more cardboard boxes. A pile of ancient-looking wooden planks were stacked against the wall.

'Stuff belonging to Aunt Win, I suppose,' her father said. 'That timber looks as if it's been here for donkey's years.'

'Poor old Aunt Winnie,' Brin said sadly. 'Fancy living here alone. It's really creepy, isn't it?' She picked up a pure white feather and sat down beside her father. 'A winter house, Toni said.' She held the feather against her mouth. Its softness was like cotton wool. Softer than anything she had ever felt before.

Her father grinned. 'She would.'

'The house is really old, isn't it?'

'There's been a house here for over two hundred years apparently. This mill would have had a scoop wheel to send the water down to the river. The dyke has long since been filled in. I expect it dried up when they built more efficient pumps further along the river. See that bit in the middle of the floor . . . ' David pointed to where the wood looked a different colour.

'Uh-uh.'

'That's where the shaft would have gone down to drive the wheel.'

'Oh. How long had Aunt Winnie lived here?'

'I don't know I'm afraid.'

'Don't you know *anything* about her?'

Brin's father shrugged. 'Very little. The solicitor said she had Alzheimer's disease. People thought she was crazy.'

'What's Al . . . Alzheimer's disease?'

'It's what old people get. And some not-so-old people, I'm afraid. It's a kind of dementia.'

'That sounds horrible.'

'Yes, it is. People lose their short term memory. They get frustrated and angry. They behave strangely. Wandering off, things like that. I suppose they do go mad in a way but it's nothing they can help.'

'Like that old gran on TV . . .'

'That's right.'

'Our gran's OK though.'

'Yes, thank God. She'd be terrible if she ever became ill. Come to think of it, she can be pretty terrible now.' David grinned down at her.

Brin smiled. Her father and Gran Ward were always having rows. Usually about politics and sex on television and stuff like that.

'I wonder what she was really like? When she was young, I mean.'

'Who—Gran?'

Brin punched her father's arm. 'No, Aunt Winnie, silly.'

'I really wish I knew. I'm really only just learning about her. All I know is she married an artist and they came to live here so he could paint. The family didn't approve . . .'

'Why on earth not?'

'I suppose being an artist wasn't respectable.'

'How silly.'

'They really cut themselves off, hardly seeing anyone for, oh . . . I don't know how many years.'

Brin frowned. 'They sound a bit . . . well, strange.'

'Oh, I don't know, sweetheart. Some people like to live a solitary life.'

Brin sighed. It wasn't hard to imagine living here in this wild and beautiful place . . . but without a family to share it with . . . ? 'I suppose so,' she said sadly.

Her father stood up. He brushed the dust off his jeans. 'Come on, you haven't been in the house yet.'

'What's it like?' Brin asked, going carefully down the stairs.

'Something else . . . a time capsule.'

Brin didn't know why, but when her father said that she felt a shiver down her spine. It was almost as if a ghost

23

walked behind her. Or perhaps it was just being inside the tower? It had a sad, heavy coldness that seemed to cast a spell over her.

Behind, her father was going on about bricked-up inglenooks and exposing beams. Brin could see they were going to live in more chaos than usual while he restored the house.

At the bottom of the stairs she glanced upward. She didn't know what made her do it. As she did, something . . . a pale shadow, moved across the light. Brin decided it must have been a cloud passing over the sun although, when they got back outside, there wasn't a single one to be seen anywhere.

4

Chris—The Snowbird

It was the end of November and the family from London were moving into Dimmocks. Chris wasn't actually spying on them. He just happened to be walking past with his fishing rods when he saw they'd arrived. They were lucky it was a dry day. It had been raining for weeks. The land was water-logged, the lane black with mud. Chris wanted to get some fishing in before the sluice at Denver was open and the level of the water went down.

Chris had already met one of the family. She'd come for the key a few weeks before. She had fairish hair, frizzy, tied up in a knot on top of her head with a red ribbon. Chris had thought she was about his age. A bit younger perhaps. Quite pretty in a pale, city kind of way.

There was a little boy running around the garden. His bright green ski jacket and trainers were covered in mud. Then there was another girl. At least Chris thought it was a girl. It was hard to tell with that Crystal Palace scarf and Day-Glo green cycling helmet. Who ever it was had darker, straight hair. It stuck out in bunches from under the helmet. The child sat huddled up on a tea-chest holding a cage with a hamster in. Sulking, Chris could tell. A woman in jeans and a black sweater came to the front door and called something. The child got up and went inside.

'Hi.'

Chris turned guiltily. 'Oh . . . hello.' He could feel his face going red. It was the girl he'd met before. She must have come from round the back.

'We're moving in.'

'So I see.'

'That's my brother, Thomas,' the girl indicated the little boy. 'Hey, Tom,' she shouted. 'Don't pull those plants up! And that one just gone indoors was my sister, Toni.'

'Why does she wear a cycling helmet?'

The girl shrugged. 'Someone gave it to her. She's crazy about it.'

'Oh.' Chris didn't really know what to say.

'She's hoping to get a bike to go with it for Christmas.'

Chris couldn't help smiling.

'Why don't you come in? Dad's threatening to make a cup of tea,' the girl suggested, smiling too. 'It's chaotic, of course, but then our house always is.'

'Er . . . no, it's OK, thanks. I'm just going fishing.' Chris waved his rods. 'Th . . . thanks anyway,' he stammered, remembering his manners.

'Dad's tea's not *that* bad.' The girl grinned again.

'No . . . It's OK, thanks.'

'Come another time then.'

'Yeah . . . all right.'

Chris knew the girl watched him as he walked down the lane. He probably looked a right twit to her eyes. Old green cagoule that had belonged to his dad. Black welly boots. Flat cap. It was no good having trendy clothes here. You just got covered in mud.

There was a car parked by the fence. When Chris looked over the stile someone had taken his favourite fishing place. He swore under his breath. He'd hoped to see the heron again. It would probably have flown off ages ago with a stranger there. Someone who didn't know how to sit quietly and blend into the landscape so nothing knew you were there but you. Chris could see a green umbrella and a couple of beer cans at the water's edge, the figure of a man sitting on a blue fishing box. Overhead, the sky hung heavy and grey. Chris thought it would probably rain again before long.

Chris put his rods on his shoulder and walked along the bank. He didn't need any fancy fishing gear. A couple of rods, bait, a few hooks. What you needed was a feel for the river. A stillness. That's what made a good fisherman.

It was late afternoon when the girl climbed the stile and came to watch him fish. He'd heard the other bloke's car roar away ages ago. It was great, sitting by the river all by yourself. Just you and the occasional moorhen. The soft feel of fine, misty rain on your face. The silence all round you. Chris loved it. There'd been no sign of the heron. He guessed the fisherman really had scared it off.

Chris tried not to scowl at the girl when she sat down beside him.

'Do you mind?'

'I'm just packing up,' he said gruffly.

'Have you caught anything?'

He shook his head. 'Nope, river's running too fast.'

The girl shivered and drew her ski jacket tightly round her. Her green wellies were shiny and new. The fine rain had darkened her hair and wisps of it stuck to her forehead.

'Is it always this cold and damp?'

'Usually.'

'Mum can't get the Rayburn going. Her and Dad are shouting at each other so I've come out.'

'My mum would show her how to light it, I expect. We've got one the same. And she used to help the old girl out sometimes. Er . . . I mean Mrs . . . er . . . your aunt.'

'Did she?'

'Well . . . she just gave a hand now and then, you know. Bit of shopping. Stuff like that.'

'By the way,' the girl said. 'My name's Brin.'

'Mine's Chris,' he mumbled, heat coming to his cheeks.

'What school do you go to?'

Chris told her.

'I'm going there too.'

'Oh . . . you'll be catching the bus then, I expect.'

That's all Chris needed. Some girl nattering all the time on the way to school. He usually used the journey to catch up on his homework.

They sat in silence. Twilight drew itself around them. A dank, grey mist was beginning to emerge like ghosts from the water. Downriver, Chris could hear the crooning of a great crested grebe as it made its way to its roost.

'Do you like fishing?' Brin asked.

'Wouldn't do it if I didn't, would I?'

'No, I suppose not. I don't like killing things.'

'I don't kill them, stupid,' Chris said contemptuously. Trust a townie to think that. 'I put them back.'

'Oh . . .'

Chris stood up. 'I'm off now.' He knew he was being unfriendly but he couldn't help it. He just hated the thought of someone coming along to spoil things every time he wanted to be alone. He could see he'd have to find somewhere else to fish. There were plenty of other places but this was his favourite.

Brin stood up too. 'Yes. I'd better get back. They've probably finished arguing by now and . . .' she broke off. When Chris looked at her she was staring upriver. She had gone quite still, pale, as if something had turned her to ice. 'Chris . . .?' He felt her hand clutch his sleeve. 'What on earth is THAT . . .?'

About a hundred metres upstream Chris saw a strange, boiling whirlpool of mist. Gradually, from its centre, a shape emerged. Shadowy. Almost transparent. On wings the colour of moonlight, it flew towards them. A sad cry came through the twilight like a long-lost funeral song. Instinctively, as the bird flew overhead, they both ducked, then turned, their eyes tracking the creature as it flew downriver. The huge wings made no sound at all in the silver-grey light of the fading day. Chris felt a cold breeze pass through his hair. Out of the corner of his eye he saw Brin's hand cover her mouth. Her eyes were round and wide in speechless surprise. The shape disappeared into the gloom. The edges of the mist seemed to draw together like a curtain behind it. The utter silence was like the aftermath of a storm.

They stood watching, waiting . . .

Chris let out his breath. He hadn't even realized he'd been holding it.

'Wow!' Brin turned to him. Her eyes shone with excitement. 'What on earth was THAT?'

Chris shook his head. He swallowed noisily. 'I don't know.' He couldn't think why he whispered.

'Its voice . . .' Brin shuddered. She wrapped her arms around herself as if winter had suddenly arrived. 'It was so sad . . .'

Stupid, but Chris felt like crying.

'Yes,' was all he managed to say.

'Was it a ghost, Chris? Do you think it was a ghost?' She was looking at him, her eyes still wide with amazement.

Chris shook his head. 'Don't be stupid . . .'

'Well, what was it then?'

'I don't . . . honestly. I . . .'

'What?'

'I've seen something like it once before,' he confessed. 'Last year. It was a lot higher up. I knew it wasn't a swan and could only think it might be a snow-goose but it definitely wasn't that either.' He shook his head. 'I looked it up in all my books but couldn't find anything like it anywhere.' Chris didn't know why he was telling her. He'd never spoken to anyone about it other than his friend Ben Smith.

'Barn owls are white, aren't they? I saw a documentary about them on TV.'

Chris looked at her in disgust. 'Don't be daft, it was enormous, much bigger than any owl.'

Brin looked hurt. 'How big do you think it was then?'

Chris shrugged. 'I don't know . . . huge . . . I reckon its wing span must have been well over two metres, much bigger than an eagle . . . bigger than anything I've ever seen.'

'It . . . looked like a Snowbird of some kind.'

Chris found his hands were shaking as he gathered up his fishing rods. 'There's no such thing as a Snowbird.'

'Well, something that lives in a snowy country. Something cold . . .' Brin shivered again.

Chris shrugged.

'Were you scared?' Brin asked.

'Nope,' Chris said, sounding braver than he felt.

'Me neither. I just felt really sad . . . I . . .'

29

But Chris was already walking towards the stile. Brin ran after him.

'Chris, do you believe in ghosts?'

''Course not,' Chris said unconvincingly.

'Are you sure you don't know what it was?' Brin had to run to keep up with him.

'No,' he said irritably. 'I told you.'

'OK,' Brin sounded hurt. 'Keep your hair on.'

Chris wished she wouldn't keep asking him. He was annoyed she'd been with him when he saw it again. Seeing it before had been like a secret he wanted to keep to himself. Ben Smith had only grinned when Chris mentioned it to him and said he must have been imagining things. Chris hadn't said any more. And he certainly hadn't heard of anyone else seeing anything like it. There were lots of local folk tales of course. About witches and will-o'-the-wisps and boggarts.

But he'd never heard one about a huge bird that flew out of the mist and scared you half to death.

At the gate, Brin said, 'Why don't you come in and meet my family now?'

Chris looked at his watch. He was surprised she was still talking to him after he'd been so rude. 'I'd better get home.'

Brin touched his arm. 'Do come in,' she said. 'You've got to meet us all some time. It might as well be now. There's no need to be shy, we're quite a friendly lot.'

'I'm not shy,' Chris protested, looking down.

'Well, come in then.'

'No,' he said. 'I can't. Not now.'

He walked on, leaving her standing at the gate. He didn't really care *what* she thought of him. All he wanted to do was get back home and search through his bird books again. He'd got a much better look this time. That's if there was such a thing as a better look at something you weren't even sure was real.

Somehow though, as he walked down the lane towards home, Chris had the peculiar feeling that if he looked in all the wildlife books in the world he'd never find this particular bird in any of them.

5

Brin—Tom's Dream

Brin's bedroom faced the river. She had been allowed first choice. There were, Brin decided, some advantages in being the oldest after all. They had kept Winnie's old brass bedstead. And a big old dressing table that would hold all Brin's clothes when she got round to unpacking them. Her mother had promised to strip and repaint the dressing table when she had time. Meanwhile a good going over with the duster got rid of the cobwebs. Brin did have to have a new mattress. The other one was stained and torn. Alex had taken one look at it, screwed up her nose and said it had got to go. Brin didn't argue.

The house had been full of old-fashioned furniture. Settees, chairs, cupboards. A huge, carved, black sideboard that took up almost all of the front room. Brin's father said there wasn't enough space for all the family *and* Aunt Winnie's furniture in the same house. They stashed some of it away in the old mill for Alex to renovate later. The rest went off to an auction. They burned all the old carpets and curtains. They were almost falling to bits anyway. Alex said they could be infested with goodness knows what. Strangely Brin felt sad, getting rid of the old lady's things. Things she'd probably treasured for years.

'I'm sorry too, Brin,' her father said. 'But they really are so grotty they're past rescuing. We've kept everything worth keeping.'

It was a couple of weeks after the family moved in that Tom started having nightmares. Afterwards, it all seemed to fit like a jigsaw puzzle but at the time Brin didn't think anything of it.

'It must be the move,' their father said. 'He'll soon settle down. You know what an over-active imagination he's got.'

The first night at Dimmocks, Brin had hardly been able to sleep. It wasn't just the excitement of moving in. She kept thinking about that bird she and Chris had seen. How it had emerged from the mist like something out of a science fiction movie. Brin tried to make a picture of it in her mind but all she could see were the huge, silent wings. All she could hear was its sad, shivering song. Brin had the strange feeling it was trying to tell them something, but what on earth it was she didn't know.

She decided to get some books from the school library and see if she could discover what kind of bird it might have been. Brin remembered she had got out of bed and gazed out of the window. She kept thinking the creature might emerge from the misty, shifting illusion of reality as it had before. But the fog had cleared and a bright, full moon shone across the water. Its reflection was like a silver ribbon. She could hear little night birds cooing and tweeting along the river, the soft lapping of ripples against the reeds. Brin waited but nothing appeared. She strained her ears but the sad-song had gone for ever.

Or so she thought.

The first time Tom had a nightmare, Brin had been sitting up in bed, reading. All the books she had been set for English were different from her old school. She'd got a lot of catching up to do. Tom's bedroom was next to hers. He shared it with Toni. Their parents' room was at the other end of the house. Brin decided they'd chosen that one on purpose so they couldn't hear the children arguing. Toni had sulked about having to share with Tom. Her mother promised she could have the room in the roof when the attic had been cleared out.

They had been exploring the old tower in the afternoon and Tom had got over-excited as usual. Brin thought probably that's why he was restless. As well as having an over-active body, Tom's mind hardly ever switched off, either. But she never remembered him having bad dreams before. Once he was asleep, he went out like a light.

The walls at Dimmocks were really thin, only lath and plaster, David said. You could hear every sound from the other side. Brin couldn't make out exactly what Tom was saying in his sleep. You hardly ever can. It's usually nonsense. She remembered when Toni was small and they shared a room. Brin never could make out what Toni was mumbling about.

Brin slipped her old sweat-shirt over her pyjamas and crept into Tom and Toni's room. The moonlight was shining across Tom's bed. It reflected tears on his little face. He was sobbing in his sleep as if someone had died. Reluctantly, Brin shook him. The last thing anyone *ever* did was wake Tom up once he had fallen asleep. Not on purpose anyway.

Tom threw up his arm and tossed around a bit. Then he opened his eyes.

'What . . . ?' he said, frowning. His eyes looked blank, as if he had been in another world and couldn't make out where he was.

'You were talking, having a nightmare,' Brin whispered.

She could see he was trying to remember.

'Not me,' Tom said.

'Yes, you.' Brin kissed his forehead and pulled his quilt straight. 'Go back to sleep now, OK?'

Tom shook his head and sat up. 'I'm getting up.'

'No, you're not. You've only been asleep a couple of hours. Look, Mum and Dad are really tired, give them a break will you, Tom?'

'Come in your bed then?'

Brin sighed. 'Tom . . .?'

'Go on,' he insisted. 'Please . . .'

She sighed again. 'OK, but you'd better be good.'

'Whoopee!'

She made him be quiet and they crept from the room. Toni was well away, her New York Giant's teddy bear tucked under her armpit.

33

Snuggled up with Brin, Tom said, 'I remember a bird.'

'What bird?'

'I dunno,' he said. 'A bird, as big as me.'

'A swan or something?'

'Dunno,' Tom said again. He tossed and turned for a while, said he was bored, then fell asleep. It was ages before Brin nodded off. She kept thinking about what Tom said.

David was getting breakfast while Alex struggled with the stove. 'Bloody thing's gone out again,' she complained.

'Chris said his mum would help you get it going.' Brin staggered into the kitchen, yawning.

'Who's Chris?'

'You know . . . . the boy up the road,' she said, yawning again and rubbing sleep from her eyes. 'The one we got the key from when we came to look at the house.'

Her father rummaged about in a cardboard box on the floor. He came up with a packet of muesli. He dumped it on the table. 'It really is about time we got this place organized,' he said irritably. 'I'm sure we could use one of those cupboards as a larder.'

'Not until it's scrubbed and painted,' Alex said.

David sighed and sat down with a piece of toast and his computer magazine.

'Is that Chris who waits at the bus stop?' Alex asked.

'Yes,' Brin said.

'He looks nice.'

'Does he?'

'Yes. You said he thought his mother would help me solve the mystery of this blasted thing.' Alex stood up. Her hair had come out of its elastic band. When she brushed it back she left a dark smudge on her nose. The front of her jeans were black with soot and ashes.

'Yes. He said his mum used to help Aunt Winnie sometimes.'

'The solicitor said the neighbours were very kind. I've been meaning to go and thank them ever since we arrived,' David said, his mouth full of toast.

'We could pop up later couldn't we, David?'

'If you like. We really should introduce ourselves, anyway. Been here two weeks and haven't seen a soul.'

'Maybe people round here don't come out in the rain.' Alex washed her hands. Brin knew she was fed up with the constant wet and mud, the cold, damp old house. She didn't complain, but Brin heard her mother and father talking. Country life wasn't as her mother expected it to be at all.

'That means they'd stay in for ever.' Brin's father grinned. 'Cheer up, Alex, it won't always be this bad. Just think, in the summer holidays you'll be lying by the river in your bikini.'

Alex smiled. 'I'll remember you said that.' She dried her hands then sat at the table. She started going through the pile of homework books that stood between the muesli and the orange juice.

In the corner, Zhivago the hamster's wheel squeaked like an army of mice.

'Can't you keep that blasted hamster somewhere else?' David said to Toni. 'That noise drives me mad.'

'No,' Toni said, looking up from the sports page of the previous day's paper. 'It's too cold anywhere else.'

'Is that why you've got your goal-keeper's gloves on?' Alex asked. 'Because you're cold?'

'No,' Toni said. 'I just like them that's all.'

Brin saw her parents exchange a smile.

Just then, Tom came into the kitchen. He had his drawing pad tucked under his arm.

'Brin said I had a nightmare,' he said, plonking himself down at the table and helping himself to cereal. 'I drew it.'

'How can you draw a nightmare, stupid!' Toni commented. She picked a wheat-flake off the back of her glove and ate it.

Tom stuck out his tongue. 'Like this.' He thrust his drawing book at her. 'So there.'

Toni screwed up her nose. 'Rubbish,' she said.

'Hey—don't be so horrible.' Brin took the pad from Toni. 'I'm sure it's very . . . ' she frowned. She turned the page upside down. 'What is it, Tom?'

'My nightmare, what do you think?'

Tom had drawn this—

$$\exists v \varnothing \varkappa \varkappa \varnothing$$
$$\nabla C / \supseteq \iota \varkappa \Delta \Pi \varnothing C v$$
$$\exists \varkappa \mu \Delta \varnothing \mathbb{C} \lambda$$

Alex looked. She smiled at Tom. 'Nice, Tom.'

'It's rubbish,' Toni said again.

Tom wasn't a bit put off. 'Well, nightmares are rubbish,' he said shovelling cereal into his mouth.

'Shut-up, you two,' their father said, frowning over the top of his spectacles.

'Can I keep it, Tom?' Brin asked.

'Yep.' Tom tore off the page. By the time it got across the table it was smeared with Marmite.

'What was your dream about, Tom?' Brin asked. 'Do you remember yet?'

'Nope. Alien monsters, I expect.' Tom jumped down from the table. 'Can I watch *Going Live*?'

Their father sighed. 'I suppose so. Damn TV's an anachronism in this house,' he mumbled.

'A what . . .?'

'An anachronism, Brin—something out of its time.'

'Oh.'

'What on earth do you want that stupid drawing for?' Toni said.

Brin shrugged. She didn't know why she wanted it. She just did.

Upstairs, Brin stuck Tom's paper on her mirror with Blu-Tack. She sat at the end of the bed and stared at it. It looked like funny Egyptian writing. The kind you get on ancient tombs. She felt sure her father would have known what it was if he hadn't been so busy reading his computer magazine. Goodness knows where Tom had got it from. Something he'd seen on TV? In one of their father's books? Who knew what went on in his Thunderbird-ridden brain-box?

* * *

'We're going along the road to see the neighbours, Brin,' her mother called from downstairs a bit later on. 'You coming?'

'What about the Littles?' Brin shouted.

'We'll only be ten minutes, they've promised to stay in and watch TV.'

At Highfen, someone was banging around in one of the machinery sheds but they couldn't see who it was. When they knocked, Wag came running from the sheds and jumped all over them.

Chris answered the door.

David held out his hand. 'Hello, you must be Chris—I'm David Collins. We've moved into Dimmocks,' he inclined his head in the direction of the house.

'He knows that, Dad,' Brin whispered, feeling stupid.

Chris shifted his feet, shook her father's hand, went red and grunted something.

'This is my wife, Alex.'

'Hi, Chris,' Alex said. 'I've seen you at the bus-stop,' she added unnecessarily.

Chris nodded and mumbled something else.

'You know Brin . . . ?'

'Mum, for goodness'sake . . . he's in my class,' Brin hissed.

Chris mumbled again and went redder. Brin's mother nudged her in the side. In certain situations Alex was inclined to get giggling fits. Brin hoped this wasn't going to be one of them. She knew Chris well enough by now to know he would die if he thought someone might be laughing at him.

'Are your parents in?'

'Er . . . yeah, Mum is . . . Come in.'

'Thanks.'

They took off their wellies and left them outside the door.

'Mum,' Chris called. 'Visitors! People from down the road.'

Chris's mother came into the lobby. She looked surprised. She took off her rubber gloves and smiled. Brin liked her straight away. Even though she could only have been about Alex's age, Chris's mother had peppery hair, tied loosely in a pony tail. Her sparkly eyes almost disappeared when she smiled. 'Come in, come in,' she said, taking off her apron.

'I'm Anne Carter. I've been meaning to come down to say hello.'

'Us too,' Alex said. Everybody introduced themselves. They were soon talking like old friends.

Chris and Brin sat opposite each other at the kitchen table. When Brin looked at Chris and smiled he went red again and pretended to be doing something with some fishing tackle.

'You two must know each other quite well by now,' Mrs Carter was saying.

'Yes,' Brin said.

'I can see the likeness,' she said, eyeing Brin up and down.

'Likeness?' What on earth was she talking about?

'To your great-aunt. She had the same shaped face and mouth as you. And I think she'd have been fair too when she was young. Although, of course, she'd been grey for years.' Mrs Carter smiled and touched her hair. 'Like me,' she said, her voice full of rue.

'Oh,' Brin said. She couldn't really see how she could look remotely like someone she didn't even know had existed until a month or two ago.

'I've been wanting to thank you, Anne,' David said. 'For your kindness to Winnie. If we'd known of her existence we would have done more ourselves.'

'Yes, I'm sure you would.' Mrs Carter shrugged. 'I didn't really do much. Just the occasional bit of shopping when the mobile grocer stopped coming round. We rescued her once or twice when she wandered off, and when she was ill I used to check on her each day. I found her . . .'

'. . . in the old tower,' Alex said.

Brin always hated it when her mother finished sentences off for people. She supposed it came from being a school teacher.

'Yes . . . poor old dear.'

'What on earth was she doing in there?' David asked. 'The place is in a terrible state.'

Mrs Carter shrugged. 'God knows.'

'Her husband used it as a studio,' Chris piped up. Everyone looked at him and he went red again.

38

'How do you know that, Chris?' Mrs Carter sounded surprised.

'She told me . . .'

'You never said so before.'

'I only just remembered.'

'It's really creepy in there,' Brin said.

'I've never been inside. I've always wanted to. Winnie always kept it locked up. I think she was scared vandals would smash it up or something.' It was the longest sentence Brin had ever heard Chris utter.

'Did you know her husband as well?' David asked.

Mrs Carter shook her head. 'No, he died years ago. Before we came here . . .'

'So you don't know anything about him?'

'Not really. Only that Winnie fell out with the family when she married him.'

'Because he was an artist?'

'I should imagine so. Not very respectable job in those days.'

Alex looked at her watch. 'Brin, why don't you take Chris to see the tower? Be careful though, I'm not too sure those stairs are safe.'

'I've said she's not to go up to the top floor again until I've looked them over,' Brin's father said.

'And just check on the Littles will you, Brin?'

It was Brin's turn to be embarrassed even though she was dying to get Chris alone to tell him about Tom's strange dream. 'Mum . . .?' she said. 'Chris might not want to . . .'

'Go on, Chris,' Mrs Carter urged. 'You've been stuck in all morning.'

All morning! Brin thought. It's still only ten o'clock.

'I was going to help Dad with the tractor,' Chris said sulkily.

'I'm sure it's not urgent,' his mother said. 'Go with Brin, there's a good boy.'

Brin saw Chris raise his eyes to the ceiling.

As they went out, Brin heard her mother asking Mrs Carter about the stove.

'I expect the chimney needs sweeping,' she said. 'I'll come and have a look if you like.'

'Oh . . . yes please.' Brin had never heard her mother sound so grateful.

'You don't have to come if you don't want to,' Brin said when they were putting their coats on. 'My mum's always being bossy . . .'

'It's OK,' Chris mumbled.

'Have you seen it again?' Brin had been dying to ask.

'Brin, you ask me that every time I see you.'

'Well, I want to know . . .'

'I'll tell you if I see it.'

'OK, OK.' Brin wondered why boys of Chris's age were so touchy.

'Maybe it won't ever come back?' she added wistfully.

'I dunno.'

Walking down the road, Brin told Chris about Tom's dream.

Chris shrugged. 'Sounds weird. Do you think it's connected with what we saw, then?'

'I dunno. It just seems strange that's all. Tom mentioning a bird.'

Chris stuck out his bottom lip. 'I'm not even sure it *was* a bird.'

'Don't be daft.'

'Well, I'm not . . . honestly.'

'What else could it be . . . a pterodactyl?'

'Now who's being daft?'

Brin thought of telling Chris about the drawing Tom had made but thought better of it. It probably wasn't connected with his dream about a bird anyway. And she could see Chris was getting annoyed, her keeping on about it.

Toni and Tom were still watching TV.

Brin put her head round the door. 'You lot OK?'

They grunted.

'This is Chris,' she said.

Toni jumped up as if she'd been shot. An empty crisp packet and half a muesli bar fell to the floor.

She grinned. 'Hi, Chris.'

'Her name's Toni,' Brin said.

'I can tell him that for myself.'

'Hello, Toni,' Chris said, grinning. He didn't go red.

'And this is Thomas.'

'Watcha, Tom.'

'Do you like Thunderbirds?' Tom said.

'Love 'em,' Chris said with a grin.

'I've got Virgil,' Tom produced the figure from the pocket of his jeans. '. . . Thunderbird 2 and 3, a calendar, a comic . . .' he waved a screwed up comic, '. . . three posters and two videos. Want to see them?'

'Er . . . not just now, thanks, Tom,' Chris said.

'Toni's got Lady Penelope.'

'No, I haven't,' Toni said. 'I swapped her for some football cards.'

'When's Dad coming back, I'm hungry?' Tom said.

'Later. You know where the grub is anyway.'

'Where you going?' Toni asked.

'I'm going to show Chris the tower.'

'I'll come.'

'No, stay with Tom.'

Toni looked sulky. 'I always have to look after him.'

'I'm coming anyway,' Tom said, jumping up.

'No, you're not. Neither of you are allowed in there.'

Toni scowled.

'Look,' Brin said, feeling sorry for her sister. 'I'll take you for a walk later, OK. We'll take some bread for the swans.'

'Big deal,' Toni said.

The key was in the kitchen. Brin saw Chris looking round. 'Does it look different in here?'

'Yes,' he said.

'None of us are very good at getting organized I'm afraid.'

'Neither was your aunt.'

Brin smiled.

41

'You kept some of her stuff then?'

'Only a bit. Most of it was sold. We've stored some furniture and things in the tower. Mum's going to renovate some of it when she gets time. Which probably means never.'

'What about the pictures?'

'What pictures?'

'The paintings her husband did.'

Brin shook her head. 'I don't know. There weren't any.'

Chris frowned. 'That's weird. They used to be all over the place. Maybe she sold them or something?'

'Maybe,' Brin said. 'Mind you there's loads of stuff in the tower we haven't had time to look at. And the attic's still full of things. Maybe she put them away for some reason.'

'She was a bit . . . well . . . er . . . crazy . . . did you know?'

'My dad said she was old and sick. She had Al . . . Alzheimer's disease.'

'What's that?'

Brin explained.

Chris nodded. 'Yep. That sounds like her.'

'Did you know her very well?'

'Quite well.'

'Tell me about her.'

Chris did. It made Brin more sad than ever to hear how lonely her great-aunt had been. How odd she had looked pushing her big old pram up and down the lane.

'The pram's in the tower—I saw it,' she said.

Chris grinned. 'It's really ancient. Falling to bits.'

'Yes, come on, I'll show you.'

Outside, the rain had stopped. The wind was blowing everything dry. It wrenched the tower door from Brin's hand as they went in. She heard it swishing up the stairs and out through the broken window on the top floor. Leaves blew about like messages someone had left scattered inside.

'Wow,' Chris looked round. 'What a mess.' He walked round looking at things, touching the walls. He turned. 'When I was a kid I used to think vampires lived in here.'

'They probably did . . . do.'

He grinned. 'Let's go up to the top.'

Brin thought how different Chris looked when he smiled. 'OK,' she said. 'Be careful though, the stairs are really wonky.'

Chris went up first. Cautiously. Testing each step.

'Boo!' Brin shouted behind him. She couldn't resist it. He looked so funny, creeping up the stairs like that.

'I suppose you think that's funny?' He scowled over his shoulder.

'Not really,' she said, grinning behind his back.

He stopped. 'Careful,' he shouted suddenly. 'It's going to . . .' He shook the handrail violently. Brin put out her hand and clutched his coat at the back.

'Chris!'

It was the first time she had heard him really laugh.

Brin was annoyed. 'I suppose you think *that's* funny.'

At the top he stopped again, one hand against the wall, one on the rickety handrail. He barred Brin's way.

'There's something up here,' he said.

'It's probably Dracula, it would serve you right.'

He turned, looking at her through his jagged fringe. He frowned. 'No . . . honestly, I'm sure I heard . . .'

'It's only pigeons. For goodness' sake let's get off these stairs . . .'

They stood at the top for a moment. Chris had been joking, there was only silence up in the mill loft. No whisper of movement, no hush of wings.

There seemed to be more mess than when Brin last went up.

'You want to block up that window,' Chris said. 'Otherwise the place'll be full of 'em, and starlings . . . right mess they make.'

The floor was littered with bird droppings and feathers. Brin walked through them to the window.

'Come and look at the view.'

Standing beside her, Chris whistled. 'It's brilliant, isn't it? You know, there used to be wind pumps all along the river,'

43

he said. 'Before they built the pumping stations. The only one left is at Wicken Fen.'

'I bet they looked beautiful,' Brin said.

They stood for a minute breathing in the view like fresh air.

'Do you like it here?' Chris asked.

'Yes, I think it's great.'

'What about your mum and dad, the kids?'

'Poor old Mum's a bit disillusioned, I think. What with all the mud and the house being so cold. Dad says she'll like it in the summer. He's an optimist, my dad.'

'She's got to get through the winter first. Going to be a hard one this year.'

'How do you know?'

Chris shrugged. 'Lots of things. Geese arriving early. Loads of redwings and field fares already . . .'

'Oh . . .'

'What do the rest of you think of it here then?'

'Dad likes it. He's got great plans for exposing beams and stuff. He's going to turn this place into an office one day. Tom likes it anywhere. Toni hates it.'

'Why?'

'She really freaked out when Mum and Dad said we were moving. She didn't want to leave all her friends.'

'Did you, then?'

'No . . . but when we first came to see Dimmocks I knew I'd be happy here.'

'Because you liked the house?'

'Not only that.' Brin bent to pick up a feather. 'I just loved the landscape. I felt . . . oh, I don't know.' She suddenly felt stupid, telling Chris those things.

'Go on . . .'

'It's just so different from anything I'm used to . . . I felt I belonged . . . you know.'

'Some people say the Fens are flat and boring,' Chris said.

Brin looked at him. 'No—they're mysterious and beautiful and there's so much space everywhere. I love the rivers, the birds . . . even the mists and rain . . . everything.'

44

'Mud . . .?'

'Well, I don't exactly love the mud,' she smiled. 'But everything else.'

'Me too.'

Their eyes met for a minute, then Chris blushed and looked away.

'This is a funny feather,' Brin said, trying desperately to change the subject.

'What?'

Chris took it from her fingers. He frowned. 'Swan's down, I think. Expect another bird brought it up here.'

'What for?'

He shrugged. 'Nesting material I suppose.'

'What, in December?' Even Brin knew birds built their nests in spring.

'It could have been up here ages.'

'No—it wasn't here when I came up before,' she frowned. 'There was another one though, I've got it in my room. I thought I'd start collecting them. Let's see if it's the same.'

Chris held the feather against his mouth, testing its cotton-wool softness.

'Come on,' Brin said. 'Let's go and get a Coke or something.'

Downstairs, Chris said, 'There's the old pram.'

Clouds of dust rose when they took the sacks off the top.

'I didn't think she had any children,' Brin said.

Chris shook his head. 'She didn't. She used it to get drift-wood for her fire and to carry shopping.'

Brin giggled. 'Funny old thing.'

The pram was rusty, almost falling to bits. Brin could see it had once been painted green. Inside, the plastic-coated cover was cracked and stained. The deep, boat-shaped body had a lid beneath where the pram mattress was supposed to go. It was divided into three sections. There was a little tab sticking up from the middle one.

'Did she put the shopping in here do you think?' Brin pulled the tab and the lid of the middle section came out.

''Spect so.'

The bottom of the pram was full of old magazines. Brin took one out. 'Oh, look.' It was called *Artists Weekly*. She gave one to Chris and picked up another.

'Wow,' he said. 'This is hilarious.'

The magazines were yellowed and fragile. They almost fell apart as they turned the pages. There were funny, old-fashioned pictures of people painting. Advertisements for paints and easels, crayons. 'A guide to Lakeland painting,' one article said. It had an ancient photograph of someone in plus-fours sitting at an easel.

'My dad would love to see these,' Brin said. 'He's mad about old magazines. He's already been through all the piles of newspapers but they're only *Daily Expresses* and ancient *Cambridgeshire Evening News*.'

She took all the magazines out from the bottom of the pram. Underneath was something else.

'What's that?'

'It's an old sketch pad I think.'

The pad was stained and damp, the edges disintegrating, the cover green and blue spotted with mildew. Brin opened it carefully. On the first two pages were faded pencil sketches of rivers flanked by pale green willows. A long, shallow boat with lots of people rowing. The Isle of Ely and the towers of its cathedral. A lock with 'Bottisham' written underneath. But when Brin turned over the last page, shock took away her breath. She thought Chris heard her gasp.

'What's wrong?' he asked.

When Brin turned to him the expression on her face must have startled him.

He frowned. 'What's up . . .? You look . . .'

'This . . .' Brin whispered. She could hardly believe her eyes. She turned the page towards Chris so he could see. 'I don't believe it. It's . . . it's Tom's dream!'

6

Chris—The Painting

Chris hadn't a clue what Brin was on about. He could see she'd gone quite pale as if she'd had some kind of shock. And when she showed him the symbols, or whatever they were, he wondered why she was making such a fuss.

$$\exists \nu \varnothing \varkappa \varkappa \varnothing$$
$$\nabla C/\supset \iota \kappa \Delta \Pi \varnothing C \nu$$
$$\exists \varkappa \mu \Delta \varnothing \mathbb{C} \lambda$$

And even when she said it was Tom's dream he still didn't know what she meant.

Then she told him.

Chris shook his head. 'Don't be daft. How can it be the same?'

'It is, it *is*,' Brin insisted. 'Come on, I'll prove it.'

Up in her bedroom Brin took Tom's drawing off her mirror. They put the two papers together.

'See!'

'Maybe Tom found the sketchbook first?'

Brin shook her head vehemently. 'No . . .' she insisted. 'He hasn't been in there. Dad's banned the little ones. We keep the tower locked.'

Chris looked at the two pieces of paper. He frowned. 'It's not some kind of computer code, is it?'

'Don't be stupid, Chris. How could my dad's great-uncle know a computer code? Or Tom for that matter?'

'Your dad's got a computer, hasn't he?'

'Yes, but Tom's not allowed to touch it.'

'Touch what?' Thomas came charging into the room.

'Dad's computer.'

47

'Don't want to anyway,' Tom said. 'What you looking at those for?' Tom knelt on the bed and peered over their shoulders.

'Do you know what these symbols mean, Tom? Is it some kind of writing?' Chris asked.

Tom shrugged and stuck out his bottom lip. 'Dunno.'

Brin took hold of him. 'Tom, *think*!'

Thomas frowned and wriggled out of her grasp. 'I don't know, Brin.' He turned to Chris. 'Do you want to see my Thunderbirds video?' He jumped off the bed and ran downstairs. 'I'll put it on,' he yelled.

Brin rolled her eyes. 'Sometimes,' she said. 'I could kill him.'

When Chris saw Brin at the bus-stop on Monday she told him her brother had had another dream.

'He was saying something about a key,' she said. She blew on her fingers to try to warm them.

'Did you ask him any more about those symbols?'

'Yes, but he still insists he's forgotten. Mind you, I don't believe him.'

'Why not?'

'If you remember a dream enough to draw something from it then you don't forget it afterwards, do you?'

'I suppose not.'

'And I'm sure he's hiding something.'

'What makes you think that?'

'Well, he usually rattles on all the time but he's quieter. Doesn't say much. Although Toni complains he talks in his sleep all night. Actually, Mum's a bit worried about him.'

'Has he always had bad dreams?' Chris asked.

Brin shook her head. 'No, up to the age of five he hardly slept at all anyway. Then we found out he was allergic to some artificial food colourings. We have to be careful what he eats. He's much better than he was.'

'Has he drawn anything else?'

'Yes.'

'What?'

'He says they're landscapes. Castles and things. Weird looking flying machines. Mum suggested colouring them in but he says they are supposed to be white. Mum says they're really good but I can hardly make them out. She's an expert at that kind of thing.'

'He *is* only little.'

'I know.'

'Have you found any of Mr Mirston's paintings yet?'

'No. Dad thinks they might be in the attic somewhere. There's loads of junk up there.'

'I can't think why she took them all off the walls.'

'What were they of?'

'All sorts of things. Views of the river and stuff. He liked winter scenes.'

'Oh . . .?'

There was silence for a minute. Then Brin said, 'Like Tom, then? I suppose "all white" must mean snow.'

'Yes.' Chris turned up his collar against the wind. He looked up at the leaden sky. 'I'm sure it *is* going to snow.'

'Really? That'll be great!'

Chris gave Brin a sour look. 'You should try living with my dad when it snows. He's still in the middle of muck-spreading.'

Brin screwed up her nose. 'We noticed. Dad wants some manure. He's going organic.'

Chris laughed. 'He's what?'

'Going organic. He's going to grow organic vegetables. He's a great one for making plans, my father.' Brin shivered and stamped her feet to try to keep warm. She glanced up at the sky. 'Maybe if it does snow we won't be able to get to school.'

'No such luck,' Chris said. 'My dad's tractor goes anywhere.'

'Well, maybe it will be the worst winter in history and we'll be cut off for weeks and weeks.' Brin stamped her feet on the grass.

'Sounds like one of Tom's nightmares.'

Brin smiled. 'It would be lovely to have a white Christmas.'

Chris wondered why girls were so stupid about that kind of thing. 'Great,' he said unenthusiastically. He leaned into the road to see if the bus was coming.

'I'm going to start sorting out the stuff in the tower at the weekend. Want to help?'

'I'm still trying to get my boat finished.'

'Oh, do come if you can. You could talk to Tom about his pictures. He likes you.'

Chris felt an unexpected sense of pleasure. He'd been trying for ages to resist being drawn into the friendly circle of Brin's family. Although he didn't really know why. Anyway, he was fighting a losing battle. Even his mother was encouraging him to spend time with them.

'It's good for you,' she kept saying. 'Having someone your own age just along the road.'

Actually, none of them were exactly his age but he knew if he pointed it out she'd take no notice.

'OK, I'll try,' he said to Brin grudgingly, not wanting to sound too keen. 'It'll be freezing in there though—like a blooming ice box.'

Chris's weather forecasting proved to be correct. It did snow that day. Sleet at first, then fine, powdery flakes. By the time the school bus arrived home in the afternoon it had turned into a blizzard. The wind blew across the Fen with an edge like a carving knife. Brin's father was there to meet them in the car.

'Hop in, Chris,' he said. 'I'll drop you off.'

'It's OK thanks, I don't mind walking.'

'Go *on* for God's sake,' Brin said, pushing him into the back.

'Don't you like us?' Toni asked.

Chris heard Brin giggle. 'Yes, 'course I do,' he said.

'Leave Chris alone,' David said.

Toni moved up closer to Chris. 'Do you play football?'

'Er . . . not in this weather.'

Brin giggled again.

'No, silly, I mean at school.'

'Yep.'

'Do you like it?'

50

'Not much.' Chris enjoyed being out of the classroom but hated all the pushing and shoving being a good football player meant.

'I do.'

'Yes, I know.'

'How do you know?'

'Your sister told me.'

'Oh . . . What *do* you like then?'

'Toni . . .!' their father warned. 'Oops!' he said as the car skidded round a bend. 'This road's dodgy.' He craned forward. 'I can hardly see where I'm going.'

'I'm only *talking* to him, Dad!' Toni whined.

'I like lots of things,' Chris said, wishing that Toni would shut-up.

'Have you got a bike?'

'Yep. It's a bit clapped out though.'

'I'm getting one for Christmas.'

'You don't know that,' Brin said from the front seat.

'Yes, I do. *And* it's going to be a mountain bike, so there.'

'There aren't many mountains in this part of the world,' Chris said, grinning.

'That doesn't matter, mountain bikes are better than . . .'

'Toni, if you don't shut-up I'll clonk you one,' her father said. 'Ignore her, Chris, she's just a nosy parker.'

Toni folded her arms and sat back in the seat, sulking.

'It's OK,' Chris said. 'I don't mind.' He looked at Thomas. 'You're quiet, Tom.'

Tom had his nose pressed to the window.

'I'm looking at the snow,' Tom said in a dreamy, far-away voice. 'I love it, it's just like . . .'

'Like what . . .?' Toni said.

'Like home . . .'

'What's he on about?' Toni said.

Brin turned from the front seat. She frowned. 'What did you say, Tommy?'

But Thomas was still staring out. His nose was pressed to the window so hard Chris could hear the air snuffling through his nostrils. 'He said it's just like home.'

51

'What's that supposed to mean?' Toni asked.

Chris said, 'London, I suppose.'

'I don't ever remember it snowing hard in London since Tom was a baby,' Brin said. 'Dad . . . do you . . .?'

But they had arrived at Highfen.

'Thanks, Mr Collins.' Chris got out. He heaved his school bag after him.

Chris stood watching as the Volvo weaved down the lane. Through air full of snow feathers he could see Tom's little face pressed to the window as if he was in a glass prison.

That day was the start of the coldest Fenland winter for over thirty years. Ice covered the lodes and the landscape became a wilderness of snow. Dimmocks and Highfen were virtually cut off from the outside world. The Collins children thought it was the most exciting thing that had ever happened to them. If it hadn't been for their father going with Anne Carter in the Land Rover to Ely for shopping they might have all starved. There were no train services for over a week and Alex had to stay with friends in London.

Sitting in the kitchen at Highfen, Ben Smith clasped his gnarled hands round a mug of tea.

'Going to be a skating match at Upware weekend.' He stretched out his stockinged feet to the stove. 'First prize a Christmas turkey.' He wiggled his toes. 'My feet's not been so frez for nigh on ten years.'

'Damned weather's getting me down.' Mr Carter was sorting out a pile of invoices on the kitchen table.

'Where's Chris got to?' Ben asked. He put his mug on the sideboard. 'Thanks, Anne, my dear, that's warmed me up a bit.'

'He's along at Dimmocks, they're clearing out the old tower.'

'Spends half his life with that family, if you ask me,' Mr Carter said.

'Oh, John, there's not much he can do around here at the moment. It keeps him out of mischief. Anyway, it's good for him to have some company of his own age.'

'Yes, I suppose you're right.' Mr Carter put the papers into a file. 'Did you want to see him, Ben?'

'I just wanted to tell him someone thought they saw a snow-goose in a flock of brents over at Wicken. Thought he might like to go out there, take a look.'

'That's unusual, isn't it?'

Ben nodded. 'Ay—could have escaped from some collection somewhere. Thought the boy'd like to see it.'

'I'm sure he'd love to.' Mrs Carter glanced at the clock. 'He should be back for his lunch soon, you can ask him.'

Just then the phone rang.

'Mum, it's me,' Chris said. 'I'm staying here for something to eat if that's OK.'

'Of course, if they don't mind.'

'No, they asked me to.'

'Ben's here, he wanted to see you.'

'I'll 'ave a word over the phone.' Ben came into the hallway.

Mrs Carter handed him the receiver.

'Jack Maynard said he saw a snow-goose over at Wicken, Chris boy. Can't remember anyone seeing one before. Fancy going out there to have a look?'

Chris drew in his breath. 'Was Mr Maynard sure that's what it was?'

'So 'e said. Fancy going?'

'Ben, I'd love to. When?'

'Tomorrow if you like.'

'Ben, that would be great. Er . . .'

'Yep?'

'Could I bring a friend . . . er . . . the girl who lives at Dimmocks now? Brin. She likes birds.'

Ben grinned. ''Course you can, Chris.'

'Thanks, Ben.'

'I'll pick you up in the Land Rover, early's best.'

'OK, Ben. Thanks, that's really great.'

53

'Didn't tell me it was a *girl* he was visiting.' Back in the kitchen, Ben grinned at Chris's mother.

'There's a girl just a bit younger than Chris, another, younger girl, and a little boy,' Mrs Carter said smiling. 'They're just friends, Ben, so don't you go teasing him. You know how sensitive he can be about that kind of thing.'

Chris came bursting through the door. He almost careered into the portable gas fire. Brin's father had taken it over to the mill-tower so Chris and Brin wouldn't freeze to death.

'I spoke to Ben Smith,' he said, out of breath. 'Someone's seen a snow-goose over at Wicken. We're going to go out there tomorrow, I . . . I said you might like to come?'

'Wow, yes I would. Is that special—a snow-goose?'

Chris looked at Brin pityingly. Didn't she know anything? 'Of *course* it's special,' he said scornfully.

'Why?'

'Well, for one thing I don't think one has *ever* been seen here before. They sometimes spend vagrant winters on the west coast but never in the Fens as far as I know.'

'Do you think that might be what we saw after all then, our Snowbird . . .?'

Chris shook his head. 'No. Definitely not. Snow-geese aren't nearly that big.'

'Maybe our bird is another rare visitor?' Brin's voice didn't sound very convincing.

'Maybe . . .'

Tom pushed open the door. 'Mum says soup's ready in ten minutes. Home made.' He came inside.

'Home made!' Brin said with horror.

Chris laughed. 'Why you saying it like that?'

'If you knew what my mum's cooking was like then you wouldn't ask.'

'It can't be that bad,' Chris said. He'd never heard of anyone's mum who couldn't cook.

'Want to bet?' Then Brin said, 'You're not supposed to be in here, Tom.'

'Mum sent me.'

'Only to tell us about lunch. Now go on back indoors —you'll freeze anyway with no coat on.'

'I'm not cold. I'm going to build a igloo.'

Brin sighed. It was a job to get Tom indoors lately. He loved the snow and never seemed to feel the cold. The line of snowmen leading down to the old boat-house was all his handiwork. His videos lay unwatched in their boxes for days on end. By six in the evening he was exhausted, ready for bed. Even his constant and recurring dreams didn't wake him up.

'*An* igloo,' Brin corrected.

'A igloo. Help me, Chris,' he tugged at the sleeve of Chris's jacket.

Chris looked at Brin.

'Well, go on,' she said.

'I'm supposed to be helping you.'

'Ten minutes won't hurt, will it? I'll just see what's in this old cupboard under the stairs, then I'll be in.'

But it was hardly any time at all before Brin came hurtling out of the door.

'Chris!' she yelled.

'We're doing a igloo,' Tom called from round the back of the tower.

When Brin found them, her cheeks were flushed with excitement. She pushed her hair from her face. She grabbed Chris's arm.

'Chris,' she said. 'Come and see . . . come and *see*.'

She dragged him away.

'Hey!' Tom protested. 'What about our igloo?'

'Chris, you must come . . . now!'

Back inside, Chris saw what all the fuss was about. The cupboard had been full of Mr Mirston's pictures. Brin had put several aside. Chris recognized a view of Baitsbite Lock that used to hang in Winnie's front room. There was one of Houghton Mill, its black timbers contrasting starkly with a

55

snowy backgound. Chris remembered it used to hang in the hall.

But it was the one Brin held in front of her that made his heart beat so fast it seemed likely to jump from his chest.

He frowned. 'What the . . .?'

He took the painting from her hands and went over to the window where the light was better.

Brin came to stand beside him. And when he looked at her, he saw her eyes were shining.

'It's her, isn't it? It's the bird we saw in the mist. Only she's not really a . . .'

'Yes,' Chris said, shaking his head in disbelief. 'It's her all right.'

'And look . . .' she whispered, pointing.

And there, printed underneath, was Tom's nightmare.

$$\exists \nu \varnothing \varkappa \varkappa \varnothing$$
$$\nabla \subset / \supset \iota \kappa \Delta \Pi \varnothing C \nu$$
$$\exists \varkappa \mu \Delta \varnothing \Phi \lambda$$

And although they hadn't heard him come in, Tom was there too, looking at the picture and smiling.

'Oh . . .' he said. 'It's you. Hello.'

7

Brin—The Snow-goose

Brin and Chris looked at one another in amazement when Tom said that.

Brin put her hands gently on Tom's shoulders. 'Have you seen her before then, Tom?' she asked. She spoke quietly although her heart was yammering in her chest. She felt on the verge of some totally brilliant discovery, although if someone had asked her what, she wouldn't have been able to tell them.

"Course,' Tom said matter-of-factly.

Over his head, Brin glanced at Chris. He was looking anxious and puzzled.

Brin took the picture from Chris. She sat down on a box and pulled Tom down beside her. He was still looking at the picture as she held it on her lap.

'Where, Tom?' she asked, trying not to sound as if her question was very important. 'Have you seen her flying in the sky?'

Tom shook his head. He frowned. 'I've just seen her in my head.'

'Do you mean in your dreams, Tom?' Chris asked softly. Brin had noticed before that he had a special way of talking to little kids.

Tom frowned again. 'I think so. She comes into my head when I'm in my bed but I don't know if I'm asleep or not.'

'And is this her name?' Brin pointed to the strange letters underneath.

Tom shook his head. 'No, it's the key, silly.'

'What key?'

Tom shrugged. 'I dunno, do I? It's just the key.'

Over his head, Chris looked at Brin and made a face.

'Does she sing to you at all?' Brin asked, remembering the sad-song that haunted her heart.

'She cries,' Tom said, sticking out his lower lip as if he was about to cry too.

Brin glanced up at Chris again. 'Why does she cry, Tom?'

'Because she's lost, dumbo.' Then he jumped up. 'I'm hungry, let's get our yukky home made soup.' He ran outside. 'Thunderbird 3 to control!' he shouted and whizzed off indoors.

Chris and Brin just looked at each other for a minute.

'What do you think, Chris?' Brin asked eventually.

He shook his head. 'I dunno.' Then he winced and shrugged his shoulders. 'He's probably been watching too much TV. It's just coincidence, Brin. What else can it be?'

'Chris, don't be daft. Look . . . Tom did that drawing after his first nightmare. Then we found the sketch in the pram. Now this . . .'

$$\exists \nu \varnothing \varkappa \varkappa \varnothing$$
$$\nabla C / \supset \iota \kappa \Delta \Pi \varnothing C \nu$$
$$\exists \varkappa \mu \Delta \varnothing \math11 \lambda$$

'. . . my great-great . . . or whatever he was, uncle, has written the same symbols under his painting of the Snow-bird . . .'

'Why do you keep calling her that?' Chris interrupted.

'Calling her what . . .?'

'A Snowbird?'

'I . . . I don't know,' she shrugged.

It was true. Brin didn't really know. All she knew was that she had begun to think of the creature they had seen that evening as a Snowbird. Not a ghost, a phantom, or any figment of her imagination. They'd *both* seen it, so how could it have been? But in spite of all that, when Brin really thought about it, she still wasn't absolutely sure if it had been there at all. There was one thing she had learned, though. At winter's twilight in this strange damp and misty land, you couldn't be sure that anything you saw was real.

'And if this isn't her name,' Brin pointed to the strange letters, 'and it's not a computer code, then what on earth is it?'

'It's a key.'

Brin thought a minute. 'No, not "a" key, Chris, "*the* key". Remember? Tom said it was *the* key.'

'The key to what?'

Brin shrugged. 'Dunno, do I?' she said in Tom's high little voice.

Chris grinned. Then, more seriously, he said, 'Look, Brin, we're asking ourselves all these questions that neither of us can answer.'

'I know.' Brin touched Chris's sleeve. 'It's scary, isn't it?' She shivered.

Chris looked round the old tower. 'I told you this place was haunted.'

'Vampires, you said.'

Chris took the painting. 'Maybe she is a vampire. A huge, white-winged vampire.'

'Not with a beautiful face like that.' Brin touched the canvas with her finger tip. Gently. As if by doing so she could touch the Snowbird to find out if she was real.

'Do you think we ought to tell someone?'

'Who?'

'Well . . . your mum . . . you said she was worried about Tom.'

'Not likely,' Brin said, sounding horrified. 'Anyway, what can we tell her? She'd think we were nutty.'

Chris shrugged. 'I suppose so.'

'Look, Chris, let's look through the rest of this stuff this afternoon. Maybe we'll find some more clues?'

'What are you going to do with the picture?'

'Put it with the other things.'

'What other things?'

'Well . . . the two papers with the symbols on and the beautiful white feathers we found upstairs.'

'Why the feathers . . .?'

They looked at each other, frowning. Then, suddenly it all became clear.

'The feathers, Chris . . . of course, the feathers!'

They both ran for the door at once. As they dashed through the house, Brin's mother called from the kitchen.

'Come on, you two, the soup's been ready ages.'

'Won't be a minute,' Brin shouted. Their feet were like drums on the uncarpeted stairs.

Brin took the feathers from her case of treasures under the bed. They laid all the things out. The feathers. The symbols. The painting of their Snowbird. All the pieces were fitting together. They even had the key to unlock the secret but there was no one to tell them how to use it.

And if someone had told them what they would discover when they did find out how to use it, never in a million years would Brin and Chris have believed them anyway.

The next morning Chris's friend, Ben Smith, took them over to Wicken Fen. They left the Land Rover by the lock-keeper's house. The sun had come out, although it was still bitterly cold. The snow was really deep and crisp, the air as cold as steel. It sparkled like diamonds. Boats moored by the lock were motionless in the frozen water. In one or two places someone had smashed the ice so the water birds had somewhere to swim. They had gathered in these lagoons, quacking and calling like football supporters.

The smell of the snow-fresh air filled Brin with a sense of excitement. Past the busy lagoons it seemed the only sound was the press and squeak of footsteps upon snow, the occasional call of a coot across the fen.

They trudged along the bank, then over a slippery wooden bridge.

'I'll lead the way,' Ben said, poking about in the snow with his stick. 'Don't want you young 'uns slipping down the bank. The ice looks pretty solid but you never know. Not walking too fast for you are we, Brin?'

"Course not,' Brin said indignantly. She saw Chris grinning behind Ben's back. She supposed Ben thought because she was a townie she wouldn't be able to keep up. Chris had admitted that he'd dreaded the family coming to Dimmocks. That somehow because they'd lived in a city they would spoil things. Maybe Ben thought town people were like that too?

'You're Mrs Mirston's niece then are you?' Ben asked.

'I think I'm her great-great-niece but I'm not actually sure,' Brin told him. 'Did you know her too?'

'Ooh, not really,' Ben said, shaking his head. 'Not me. But the wife's mother used to visit Dimmocks when she was a young girl.'

'I didn't know that,' Chris piped up.

'No reason why you should, boy. It was all long before your time.'

'Did she know my aunt's husband?' Brin asked.

'I suppose she must 'ave done. Why d'you want to know that?'

'I just wondered . . . we only know a little bit about Aunt Winnie and nothing at all about her husband. I've often wondered what he was like.'

'Oh, I see.' Ben strode on ahead. Brin noticed the cold had nipped the tips of his ears and turned them red.

She kicked through the snow and caught up with him. 'Is she still alive?'

'Who?'

'Your wife's mother.'

'Bless you, no. Been dead years.'

'Oh . . .'

Brin thought she must have sounded disappointed because Ben said, 'But I'm sure the wife would have a tale or two to tell if you asked her. Get young Chris 'ere to bring you over sometime. Eh?'

'Oh, yes please. Chris, will you?'

But Chris had lagged behind. They waited. He had something in his hand.

'Moorhen's feather,' he said. 'Looks as if something got hold of it.'

'I hope it got away.'

'Looks like it.'

Brin took the glistening black feather from Chris's hand. She smiled at him. 'Can I have it for my collection?'

Chris shrugged. He went a bit red. Brin hadn't seen him do that for ages. 'If you want,' He said indifferently. He glanced at Ben.

'There must be so many different species of birds here,' Brin said, putting the feather carefully into her pocket.

'It's a wildlife sanctuary,' Ben said. 'The oldest one in the country.'

'Yes, my dad told me.'

'You want to come along here in the summer,' Chris said. 'Get eaten alive by mozzies.'

'Mozzies?'

'Mosquitoes. It's famous for it.'

'Oh.' Brin thought she'd rather freeze than get eaten alive by mozzies.

In places, the raised footpath along the lode had almost disappeared beneath deep drifts. A line of animal tracks led to a bloodstained hollow in the snow. A few brown feathers lay around its rim.

'See,' Chris said grimly. 'Hunting's easy for foxes this weather.'

Brin was glad the feathers weren't white.

Across the water, sedges looked like frayed banners waving in the wind. Snow hung on willow branches like washing. It was so beautiful it took away Brin's breath. She pulled her hat down over her ears and kicked the snow into little blizzards in front of her. Her face was numb with cold. Her toes were like ice cubes.

'Where was the snow-goose sighted?' Chris asked excitedly.

'Along near the keeper's lodge. We can use the hide.'

The next half hour was spent almost freezing to death in a wooden hut with viewing windows just big enough to look through. There were huge flocks of birds coming and going, skidding as they splashed down on to the ice-free lagoons like aircraft out of control. Ducks, swans, geese, Chris could name each one.

'That's a flock of grey-lags,' he whispered.

'Aren't they noisy?' Brin commented as honking cries echoed over the snow. 'They sound like the first form at break.'

Chris gave her a withering look. '. . . and they're white fronted geese,' he went on, '. . . and they're Bewick's swans, look, you can see the little yellow bit above their beaks. Whooper's have more yellow than that.'

'Do you know the names of all of them?' Brin asked. She was impressed, although she didn't let on.

'Yep.'

'Big 'ead.'

Chris looked at her and went a bit red again. Brin heard Ben snort with laughter then cover it up by lighting his pipe and puffing away like a chimney.

'You'll know the snow-goose then? If it comes?'

'Don't be stupid. 'Course I will.'

Then Brin heard Chris draw in his breath. He clutched Ben's arm and pointed. 'There it is!' He held his binoculars up to his eyes. 'Amongst that flock of dark breasted brents . . . look!'

Ben put his pipe down hastily on the ledge and looked through his binoculars. 'You're right, boy. Want to look, young lady?' Ben handed the glasses to Brin.

'Can you see it, Brin?' Chris asked excitedly.

She nodded.

As a flock of dark-breasted geese circled, then landed, Brin saw, in their midst, a pure white bird. Its black wing tips were shiny, like jet, its red bill a splash of blood against the sky. Brin held her breath. The bird was beautiful, smaller, more elegant than its companions. More graceful. As the brents came in to land amid a scurry of beating wings and honking cries from the wildfowl already on the water, the snow-goose circled once. It seemed as if it wanted to make an entrance all of its own, just for the watchers' benefit. It settled

63

with hardly a splash and disappeared amongst the host of other species jostling for space on the surface.

Brin lowered the glasses and let out her breath. 'Wow.'

Chris was looking really chuffed. 'Thanks for bringing us, Ben. I never really thought I'd ever see one here. It's unreal, isn't it, Brin?'

'Yes—it . . . it's beautiful. Does it stay here all year?'

'No, no,' Ben said. 'They come from North America but as this one's got tied up with a flock of brents it may go further north . . . back to Arctic Europe with them.'

'It could have escaped from a wildfowl collection in Britain,' Chris piped up. 'There's no way of telling.'

'One thing's for sure,' Ben said. 'It's got lost. I doubt it will ever find its way home. You get that sometimes . . . a bird never finding its way back to its native habitat.'

Then, as if he suddenly realized what Ben had said, Chris stared at Brin.

'Yes . . .' he said thoughtfully. 'It must have got lost . . .'

8

Chris—Something Shiny

A few days later, Chris had a phone call from Brin.

'Chris, can you come over?'

'I'm supposed to be helping my dad this morning.'

'Please . . . it's really important.'

'OK, I'll try and come later.'

It was three o'clock, the light fast fading, before he finally made it.

Brin answered the door. 'They've all gone Christmas shopping,' she told him.

Chris hung his coat by the Rayburn. 'Didn't you want to go?'

'I wanted to see you. I wanted to tell you Tom had another dream,' Brin said. 'A really weird one this time. Mum's thinking about taking him to the doctor's after Christmas.'

'Is he ill then?'

'Not really ill. Just not himself . . .'

'How do you mean?'

'Well . . . although he's naughty like all six year olds he was *really* bad today.'

'What did he do?' Chris imagined a variety of things from smashing the best china to tearing up Toni's poster of Crystal Palace Football Club.

'Well, against Dad's strict orders he went into the old tower.'

'That's not so bad, is it?' Chris thought it all sounded a fuss about nothing.

'I didn't think so really but I suppose if he'd fallen down the stairs or something he could have been killed. Mum tends to be a bit over-protective since . . .'

'Since what . . .?'

'Since she lost a baby.'

'Oh?'

'Dad says it's because Tom's the youngest, still a baby in a way, I suppose.'

Chris thought of all the things he did when he was Tom's age. Riding on the tractor, pedalling his bike to school in the village, climbing trees, making camps along the river. Nothing over-protective about his parents, that's for sure. He supposed that's what became of being a townie.

'What did he go in the tower for, did he say?'

'He told Mum he was looking for someone.'

Chris frowned. 'How weird.'

'Yes. And he cried like anything when Dad told him off. He doesn't usually bat an eyelid.'

'Poor old Tom.'

'And besides all that, he's really tired the whole time and that's unknown in the history of his life.'

'Maybe he's just excited about Christmas.'

Brin shook her head. 'No, it's more than that.'

'Poor old Tom,' Chris said again. 'What was his dream about, anyway?' Chris wished Brin would get on with it. The suspense was killing him.

'Well, Toni was moaning about being kept awake so I took Tom into my bed.' Brin made a face. 'It's no joke I can tell you, getting up in the middle of the night in this house. It's as cold as an Arctic expedition upstairs . . .'

'I bet.'

'Anyway, I lifted Tom out and he hardly woke up at all. He just kept mumbling stuff.'

'What kind of stuff?'

Brin frowned. 'Actually, it *was* a bit mixed up but mostly he was going on about dying. He was crying like anything in his sleep and he kept asking if I could set the key?'

Chris frowned. 'I wonder what he meant? Did you ask him?'

'Yes, I asked him to tell me *how* to set the key. Whatever that means.'

'What did he say?'

66

'Nothing, he was just going on about a last flight or something. It was really weird.'

'Doesn't make much sense to me.' Chris frowned. 'In fact it sounds like a load of old rubbish. You sure Tom's not having you on, Brin?'

'No, of course not, Chris. If you could see him having one of these nightmares you'd know I was telling the truth. He looks . . .'

'What?'

'Really sad, I mean as if he really was dying,' she shuddered. 'It gives me the creeps I can tell you.'

To Chris's horror Brin looked as if she was going to cry. If she did, he didn't know *what* he would do.

'His pillow was soaked with tears,' Brin went on. Her voice sounded rather peculiar. 'It made me want to cry too. The noise he made reminded me of . . .' Brin hesitated.

'Of what?'

'I know it sounds daft, but it reminded me of the noise the Snowbird made when we saw her by the river. That sadsong. Do you remember?'

'Yes, 'course I do. How could I forget?'

'Chris, she's trying to tell us something . . . through Tom. I know it.'

'Don't be stupid. How could . . .?'

'Honestly, I think she's using him as a kind of . . . well a kind of transmitter. Oh, Chris, I know it sounds daft . . .'

'OK, if that was true, and I mean *if*, why Tom? Why not you . . . or Toni?'

Brin shrugged. 'I don't know. Maybe because he's so young, his mind is . . . well, open to suggestion, if you like.'

Chris sighed. 'You've been watching too many of those horror films, Brin.'

'I haven't. I'm hardly ever allowed to.'

Chris shook his head. 'I honestly don't believe in all this ghost stuff. I used to when I was a kid but not now.'

'Me neither . . . not really. But something's giving Tom strange dreams. And it's something to do with the Snowbird, I know it.'

'But we don't even know if it's real, do we? I mean it was so misty, getting dark . . .'

'She must be real. Winnie's husband saw her . . .'

'We don't know that. He could have just made her up.'

'Chris, for goodness' sake. You know that would be too much of a coincidence. Tell me how Tom could have recognized the painting, then?'

'I don't know,' Chris admitted.

'Chris, that's four of us. You, me, Tom, and Uncle whatever-his-name-was. We've all seen her.'

Chris shook his head again then brushed his hair from his eyes. 'Snowbirds, nightmares . . . I don't know, Brin. It all sounds a bit OTT to me. And anyway, I *know* about birds . . .' Chris broke off. Brin was staring at him with a weird expression on her face.

Then she said, 'Chris, you know as well as I do that she isn't really a bird.'

Chris looked away. It was something he'd hardly allowed himself to think about. Only at night, in bed, when nothing but silence echoed across the frozen, snowlit Fen did he let his mind dwell on it. He thought about the hours he'd spent searching through his encyclopaedia of birds. Every known species on the earth was in there. Every one but . . . Even then, Chris still refused to believe what his eyes had told him that evening down by the river. And that other time, that other misty night when he had seen her emerge from the mist like something from another . . . No, it was just too stupid to think about.

Chris got up and paced the room. He decided to ignore what Brin had just said. Avoiding the issue, his father would call it. Something Chris was good at when questioned about his school work.

'Well . . . OK,' he said eventually, unable to ignore Brin's questioning gaze any longer. 'If what you say is true, how on earth can we find out what she is trying to tell us . . . or you . . .?'

'It's not just me. She's trying to tell anybody who'll listen. Maybe she tried to tell my great-uncle . . . or Aunt Winnie.'

'Well, the old girl *was* always talking to herself . . . maybe . . .'

'See . . . you're beginning to believe it, too.'

'I didn't say that.'

'No, but I can see you are.'

'OK, you tell me how we can find out then?'

'I'm sure the answer's in the mill-tower. That's why I wanted you to come over . . . so we could go and look.'

'Why do you think the tower's got anything to do with it?'

'Because every time Tom goes in there he has a nightmare. Even Mum and Dad noticed. That's one reason why the kids were banned.'

'I thought that was because it's unsafe.'

'That as well. I suppose they think going in there's frightening him.'

'How can you be frightened by a stupid old tower when you're mad about alien monsters and things?'

Brin smiled. 'They're not real, are they?'

'That's true.'

'And that place is definitely spooky. We both agreed. All those noises upstairs . . .'

'It's only pigeons.'

'Is it, Chris? Are you sure?'

'Well, you've been up there more than me. Have you seen anything weird?'

Brin shook her head. 'No, but . . .'

'But what?'

'Chris, there's so much junk up there, something could be hidden . . .'

'OK, we'll look then.'

Chris glanced up above the Rayburn where Brin's mother had hung the view of Houghton Mill. The picture looked so realistic Chris could almost feel the sting of cold air on his face and hear the water foaming through the mill-wheel like thunder. Brin's ancestor had certainly been a brilliant artist. If he had drawn the Snowbird from real life, then you could bet anything that's what she really looked like.

Brin jumped up. 'Let's go now.'

'Brin, it's almost dark. And it'll be freezing.'

'I don't care. We'll take a torch. Come *on*, Chris.'

Brin began putting on her coat. She wrapped Toni's Crystal Palace football scarf round her neck. Reluctantly Chris put his coat on too. He zipped it up to the top.

'Here . . . ' Brin took a torch from the cupboard.

'We'll need more than one.'

Brin waved another torch at him. 'No problem.' She switched it on and off to test the battery.

'Brin . . .?'

'Chris, if you don't want to come with me you needn't. Not if you really don't want to. I'm quite capable of looking after myself.'

But Chris couldn't let her climb those wonky old stairs alone on a freezing, dark evening. If she fell, no one might find her for hours. It would be like poor old Winnie all over again. Chris wondered fleetingly if that's what Mrs Mirston had been doing. Climbing the stairs of the old mill-tower at night to look for a clue to a mystery that she hadn't been able to solve either.

'Of course I'll come,' he mumbled. 'What do you think I am?'

'I thought you might be scared,' Brin said, grinning. She shut the kitchen door behind them.

'Who me?' Chris tried to sound joky but didn't know if he'd succeeded or not.

Brin had forgotten the key and had to go back for it. Chris stood staring at the tower. It looked black against the heavy, darkening sky. The ivy like some dark stain across its face. The broken window was an eye looking at him. He had just begun to imagine something moved behind it when Brin appeared with the key.

She unlocked the door and pushed it open. She shone her torch inside. Above, the usual rustlings of mice and birds sounded loud in the torchlit silence.

'Come on,' she whispered.

'Why are you whispering, Brin?'

Brin shrugged. Then grinned. 'Don't know. Why are you?'

Brin went up first. She flashed the torch up into the hatchway. Whatever had been moving about up there was now still. Close behind, Chris shone the torch on to the stair-treads.

'You start over there,' Brin said when they reached the top. 'I'll start with this pile of cardboard boxes.'

'You're pretty bossy you know,' Chris remarked.

'Sorry. It's being the eldest, I suppose and my mum telling me women should be assertive.'

Chris raised his eyebrows and sighed.

After ten minutes Chris was fed up. His nose and mouth were full of dust and his hands felt as if they had dropped off. The air in the tower was so cold it was like breathing in drawing pins. The torchlight threw strange shadows that he tried to avoid looking at. Once he stopped searching and looked out of the window. In the silver snow-light, the Fen looked like an endless, alien landscape.

He shivered. 'We'll get frostbite if we stay here much longer.'

By the light of his torch he saw Brin stand up, hands on hips.

'Chris, do you want to solve this mystery or not?'

'I suppose so,' he mumbled.

But before long Brin lost heart, too. 'It's no good, Chris, there's nothing here,' she said dejectedly. 'Just rubbish and old birds' nests.' She brushed at her jacket. 'I'm filthy.' She sneezed violently.

'What do you want to do then?'

'I suppose we'd better go back in before we die of exposure,' Brin said reluctantly.

She sounded so disappointed Chris felt sorry for her. Awkwardly he put his hand on her shoulder.

'Look, Brin, if there's anything here I'm sure we'll find it. It's better to come in daylight.'

He heard Brin sigh. 'OK, you're right, I suppose. But I'm going to try to come back tomorrow.'

'Tomorrow's Christmas Eve.'

'I don't care.'

At the top of the stairs Chris flashed his torch once more around the tower room. He thought it strange the beam picked up no sign of roosting pigeons. He'd have thought there would be at least a few spending the winter sheltered here. He knew lots of birds had died of starvation during the bitter spell of weather. Small birds especially. But pigeons were better at keeping warm . . .

Behind the pile of old planks stacked against the wall something suddenly gleamed, catching the torch-light like silver.

'Hang on a minute, Brin.'

Brin turned. 'What?' By the light of her torch, Chris could see her breath coming out in a wreath of grey.

'I dunno. The torch just picked something up . . .'

'What?'

'It's probably nothing. I'll just go and look.'

'I'm coming too.'

Chris crouched down in front of the stack of timber. He screwed up his eyes and tried to peer in between the planks. Something, he couldn't make out what, gleamed like moonshine.

'Chris, what *is* it,' Brin hissed from behind.

'I don't know, something shiny.'

'Let's move the planks then.'

Chris stood up and began helping Brin. Once or twice splinters caught his skin and he swore under his breath.

'There *is* something there,' Brin said excitedly. 'I can see it. It looks like a huge . . .'

Just then, the wide beam of car headlights swept into the drive below. They heard voices, the slamming of car doors.

'Oh, bum!' Brin exclaimed. 'It's Mum and Dad and the Littles. Dad'll have a fit if he knows we're in here.'

'Quick,' Chris hissed. 'Put the planks back.'

'Why . . .?'

'Just put them back!'

Hurriedly they re-stacked the timber against the wall.

'Come on!'

72

Brin and Chris crept quickly down the stairs. Outside, Mr Collins was unloading carrier bags from the boot. Brin held her finger to her lips and peered round the door. Chris heard the front door of the house slam shut. Then, through the front room window, he could see someone had switched on the Christmas tree lights. He thought how strange it was that rooms looked quite different viewed from the outside through a lighted window. Somehow mysterious and strange, more exciting than they really were.

Brin pulled his sleeve. 'Come on, let's go in.'

'What shall we say we were doing?'

'Bird watching.'

'What, in the snow . . . in the dark?'

'Why not?'

Chris shrugged. 'Why not,' he said. 'If they believe that, they'll believe anything.'

9

Brin—The Photograph and the Key

The day after Christmas, the Collins family went to Chris's house for drinks. It felt like something out of a Christmas card, trudging through the snow to spend Boxing Day with neighbours. Only it wasn't quite as romantic as that. The snow had turned black where vehicles had driven along the lane. The tyre ruts were stone-hard and difficult to walk on. Twice, Toni fell off her new mountain bike and had to be picked up and brushed down. A freezing wind blew across the Fen. It was so cold it seriously threatened to kill them all before they reached Highfen. Even Tom kept complaining his feet were cold and asking why they hadn't taken the car. David hoisted him on his shoulders to shut him up.

'I'm a giant, I'm a giant,' Tom shouted. He waved his pink-mittened hands around. His father slipped, almost lost his balance.

'F.A.B.' he muttered under his breath.

'Yes,' Toni said, waiting for the others to catch up. 'A giant pain in the neck.'

Toni was in a good mood for a change. In fact everyone hoped the arrival of the mountain bike would see a change in her personality. Alex told Brin she should be patient with her. She was taking a long time to settle in the new house. Brin did try. The only thing that had threatened to spoil Toni's Christmas day was getting a book about Tottenham Hotspurs from Gran Ward. Their father said he felt sure Gran wouldn't be offended if they changed it.

It seemed Mrs Carter had been cooking for months. The table was laden with sausage rolls, sandwiches, vol-au-vents, ham, and salads. She'd even laid a special little table for Tom. On it was a home-made jelly.

'Nothing artificial in it,' she said, giving the small boy a hug.

At the end of the big table was a Christmas cake with candles and a sprig of real holly on the top.

'Wow!' Toni said, her eyes almost popping from her head. Brin always said Toni was a real pig when it came to food. She even liked their mother's cooking. Sometimes.

'Toni!' Alex warned. Smiling, she handed Mrs Carter a cake tin full of mince pies.

Brin made a face at Chris. 'They're home made,' she whispered. 'The mince has all run out and stuck to the pastry. They taste really yukky.'

Chris grinned.

Mrs Carter said thanks and took the tin into the kitchen. She came out minutes later with the mince pies on a plate. She told everyone to help themselves to anything they wanted. So Toni did. Carefully avoiding her mother's mince pies she took a couple of sausage rolls, a handful of crisps and a chocolate marshmallow.

'Umm,' she said. 'Yummy.'

'Are you expecting the whole neighbourhood?' David asked, grinning.

'Just Ben Smith and his wife, Marjorie. They'll be here soon I expect.'

Just as she said that they turned up at the door. After the introductions, Brin managed to drag Chris off to the kitchen.

'Have you had a chance to go back into the tower?' he asked. Brin could see he was as anxious as she was to solve the mystery.

She shook her head. 'Not a hope. But they're all going to visit my gran tomorrow and I'm staying at home. We could go then.'

'How'd you manage that?'

'Said I've got a school project to catch up on. It's true actually, I have. We've been given loads of stuff to do in the holidays. But it'll only take me a couple of hours. If you could come over we'll find out what's behind those planks, OK?'

'Great,' Chris said.

Brin heard her father call from the front room.

He was sitting by the Christmas tree with Brin's mother, Mrs Smith, and Anne Carter. The others were watching football on TV. Except Tom. He was on the floor playing with his new Brains figure. He must have smuggled it in his coat pocket. Tom's Thunderbird figures had a way of appearing from various parts of his clothing as if by magic.

'Mrs Smith thought we might like to see these, Brin,' Alex said.

'What are they?'

'A few photographs I found amongst my mother's things,' Mrs Smith explained. 'Ben said he'd told you she used to visit Dimmocks as a child. I thought you might be interested to see them?'

'Oh, great!' Brin said, looking over her father's shoulder. He was gazing at a photograph of a young woman in a long dress sitting in a flat kind of boat.

'Who's that?' Brin asked.

'It's Aunt Winnie.' Her father had a sad look on his face. 'She was pretty, wasn't she?'

Brin took the picture from him. She touched it gently as if she could feel the texture of Winnie's floral dress. 'Yes,' she said feeling sad too. 'She was.'

'Let's have a look,' Mr Carter said from in front of the TV.

Brin took the picture to show him.

'Doesn't look much like her to me,' he said, handing it back.

'It was taken many years before we knew her,' Mrs Carter said. 'She always seemed old to us, I'm afraid.'

Brin took the photograph back to the table. Mrs Carter picked it up. She peered closer. 'She's got that locket on,' she said.

'What locket?' Alex examined the picture again.

'The one she always wore. She had it on the day before her accident.'

'Oh . . . ?

Mrs Carter shook her head. 'I do wish I knew what happened to it. I told the solicitor about it. I don't suppose you've come across it, have you?'

Alex shook her head. 'No, there's nothing like that in the house. At least, not that I know of. There's still a lot of stuff in the loft we haven't got round to turning out yet.'

'Maybe you'll come across it. It's a shame if it's got lost though. I imagine it was quite valuable.'

'Perhaps the chain got broken when she fell?'

'I think I would have found it if it had. And it certainly wasn't amongst the clothes she was wearing when they took her to hospital. They would have returned it if it had been.'

'Maybe it'll turn up,' David said.

Mrs Smith showed them the other photos. One or two were of the house when it was in a better state of repair. One of a couple on old bone-shaker bicycles cycling along the lane. Their backs were towards the camera but Mrs Smith said she thought it was Aunt Winnie and her husband.

'What was his name?' Brin asked.

Mrs Smith frowned. 'It was Jacob, I think.' She turned the photograph over but there was nothing written on the back. 'Yes . . . I'm sure it was Jacob . . . '

'Do you know anything about him? He seems a bit of a mystery.'

'No, I'm afraid not,' she took another picture from the envelope and handed it to Brin. ' . . . and here's another one of them in the garden. You see,' she added, 'they didn't always live like hermits.'

The scene was like something you see in those old black and white movies on television. People sitting in the garden. There were several women and a teenage girl in a wide straw hat, sitting at a wicker table with cups and saucers and a teapot on it. The men were draped around them on the grass. Some wore white trousers and straw boaters. Three flat-bottomed boats were moored to the landing stage beside the boat-house. Flowers danced along the borders of the lawn. Behind, you could see the mill-tower. The door was open.

Chris was looking over Brin's shoulder. She heard him whistle softly. He took the photograph from her and held it towards the light. Then he handed it back.

'See that?' he said, pointing.

Along the river, something blurred flew.

Before Brin could comment, her father piped up.

'It's a swan or something. It must have taken off just as the picture was being taken. Looks weird, doesn't it. Like a ghost,' he grinned.

'Don't say that,' Alex frowned. 'You'll frighten Tom.' But Tom was busy fighting an imaginary battle under the table.

Toni tore herself away from the TV to come and look.

She frowned, then looked closer. 'What's that?' she pointed at the blurred figure.

'A swan or something,' her mother said.

'Looks more like an angel. See . . . ?' Toni pointed. 'It's got a face.'

'Don't be daft, Toni,' David said. 'I tell you it's a . . . ' He looked closer. 'I don't know . . . it is rather big.'

Toni shrugged. 'Well, it must be a giant then.' She helped herself to some cheese straws and a pickled onion and went back to the television.

'What do you think it is, Chris?' David said. 'You're the expert.'

Chris peered at the photograph again for a minute or two, then shrugged. 'I dunno what it is, I'm afraid.' He looked at Brin and handed the photograph back to her father. Chris had hardly said a word since the Collinses arrived but they had got used to him being the silent type. Alex said it was quite refreshing to know a young person who didn't talk non-stop.

'It's the angle of the camera making it look that size.' Brin's father passed the photo to his wife. 'What do you think, Alex?'

'I don't know. It could even be a fault on the negative. But it is a lovely photograph.' She pointed to a woman seated at one end of the table. 'Winnie has the same dress on as in the other picture. And she's wearing her locket.'

'Yes, and that's my mother.' Mrs Smith pointed to the girl.

'I love those thirties fashions, don't you?' Mrs Carter remarked.

'Yes.' Mrs Smith looked at Brin. 'Girls looked like girls in those days.'

Brin saw her mother glance in her direction. She hoped her mother wasn't going to giggle. Brin put her hand over her jeans where they were torn at the knee and thought how awful it must have been to have to go around in a dress and stockings all the time.

'It looks like the frock she wore when I took her out in my boat,' Chris said. 'It was all crumpled up as if it had been folded up for years.'

'Poor old thing,' Mrs Carter's voice was sad. 'What a way to end your life.'

They all sat in silence. Brin knew they were thinking about poor old Winnie.

Except her and Chris. *They* were thinking about something else entirely.

'I don't suppose I could have this photo, could I please?' Brin held up the one with the people sitting on the lawn.

'Brin . . . ?' her mother said.

Mrs Smith smiled. 'It's all right, Alex, of course she can have it. I'm sure my mother would have wanted her to.'

'I could find a frame for it and put it in my room,' Brin said.

But there were other reasons she wanted it.

Reasons the adults would never have dreamed of.

Later that night, Brin sat up in bed looking at the photograph. She pulled the edges of her father's old woolly cardigan closer together for warmth. She had asked for a dressing gown for Christmas but had got a new track suit and trainers instead. And a personal stereo that she'd wanted since she was about six. Brin thought probably her father's old cardie was just as warm as a dressing gown anyway. Just not quite so elegant.

Amongst her bedroom chaos, Brin had managed to find the magnifying glass she used to use for her stamp collection. She examined the bird in the photograph. It definitely wasn't a swan. And it wasn't even really blurred. It *looked* blurred because it was almost transparent. And through the magnifying glass she could just make out its face.

Brin picked up a book from her bedside cupboard and tucked the photograph inside to keep it flat. The book was the one of Fenland Tales her mother had given her ages ago. She never had got round to reading it. She flicked idly through the pages. A story about a bitterly cold fenland winter caught her eye. 1799 it said. Almost two hundred years ago. That would be about the time Dimmocks was built. Brin moved her bedside lamp so she could see better and snuggled down under the duvet to read.

Next morning, Brin heard her mother call from downstairs. 'We're leaving now, Brin. I'll ring later to see if you're OK.'

Brin emerged from the bedclothes. She struggled out. She shivered. Her toes curled up from the coldness of the bare boards. She ran to the top of the stairs.

'OK, Mum. Give my love to Gran. Tell her I'm sorry I couldn't come.'

'You sure you'll be all right?'

''Course I will.'

'There's some cold turkey in the fridge,' her father called.

'Thanks.' Brin didn't actually think she could face any more turkey for at least another twelve months. 'Have a good time,' she called. 'Tell Gran I'll write to thank her for the sweat-shirt.' The front door slammed. Brin could hear Tom and Toni arguing as they got in the car.

Brin scraped the ice off the inside of her bedroom window and waved goodbye. She didn't think they could see her but it made her feel less guilty about not going.

Tom had been the worst one.

'Oh, come on, Brin,' he'd said, pulling her duvet off earlier that morning. 'It'll be so boring at Gran's without you.'

Brin had wrenched the cover back. 'I can't, Tom. I've got loads of homework. Honestly you'll have great fun. Gran's taking you out for a meal.'

'I hate going out to eat.' He made an evil face. 'Yuk!'

Brin had sat up and given him a hug. 'It'll be lovely, Tom, we've got all the rest of the holidays together haven't we? You've promised me a go on the sledge Santa Claus brought you, remember?'

Tom had nodded reluctantly.

'Come on, Tom,' Toni had called. 'Dad's got breakfast. We'll be late if you don't come now.'

In spite of the Spurs football book, Toni loved going to Gran Ward's. She always had a little dish of sweets on the table that Toni could scoff whenever she wanted.

Downstairs Brin sat by the Rayburn in her father's old cardigan and her green pyjamas. She finished the book over a peanut butter and strawberry jam sandwich. She stretched and yawned. She thought how wonderful it was to have a whole day to herself.

There was a knock at the door.

'Who is it?' Brin called, looking down at her pyjamas in horror.

'It's only me.'

She opened the door a fraction. 'Chris, you're early.'

'I know. I've got to help Dad later . . . '

She let him in. He looked at her clothes and grinned.

Brin gave him a haughty look and did a twirl. 'I'll have you know green pyjamas and a vomit-coloured cardigan that used to belong to your dad are very trendy.'

'No kidding?' Chris said, not even going red.

Brin ran upstairs to get dressed. When she came down Chris was looking at the book of Fenland tales.

'This yours?'

'Mum's actually but I've just read it . . . '

'Is it good?'

'It's OK. Some of the stories are a bit creepy. You can borrow it if you like. I'm sure Mum won't mind.'

Chris put the book down. 'I'm not much of a one for reading these days,' he said. 'Used to when I was a kid.'

'Well, I'll tell you about them sometime. Come on, let's get going.'

'Don't forget your gloves. Those planks are full of splinters.'

Outside there were no signs of a thaw. Brin thought of the story she'd been reading about that dreadful winter all that time ago. Lots of people and animals had frozen to death. One poor woman was trapped in the snow for eight days when she fell off her horse. Brin shivered. She looked up at the tower. Against the heavy, grey sky it looked forbidding. Suddenly she felt scared of what they might find. Supposing there was something evil in the tower . . . Supposing . . . ?

'Come on,' Chris said impatiently. 'I've only got a couple of hours.'

Brin unlocked the door and pushed it open wide.

'You go first,' she said.

Chris looked at her. 'You scared?'

She shook her head. 'No . . . not really. I just felt a bit apprehensive.'

'You were OK before and it was dark then.'

'I know. I just . . . it's probably that book I've been reading.'

'We don't have to look if you don't want to.'

'No, we've got to find out what's behind those planks. Come on.'

Upstairs the planks were in the same, hurriedly stacked pile they had left the day before Christmas Eve. They moved them carefully and re-stacked them against the opposite wall.

'I can see it,' Chris said excitedly. 'I knew there was something here. I knew it.'

They took away the last of the wood.

Brin didn't know how long they both stood, staring. Afterwards Brin remembered she suddenly became aware that her hand held Chris's arm. She didn't know how it got there. Usually he'd move away and turn a bit red. This time he had just stood there, beside her, holding his breath.

In front of them, silver-grey, half hidden in shadow, was a huge and perfect egg. Brin didn't know what it was made of. All she knew was its surface looked smooth as silk and that they could just see themselves. Small, distorted reflections —misty, like tiny, speechless ghosts.

It was the most beautiful thing Brin had ever seen in her life.

Brin knelt down. She took off her glove. She stretched out her hand. All she wanted to do was touch it.

'No . . . !' Chris tried to pull her back. 'No . . . don't . . . '

But she already had.

'It feels freezing.' Brin didn't know why she was whispering. 'Smooth and beautiful as ice.'

Brin felt Chris kneel down beside her. He put out his hand and touched the egg too. Tentatively. Then he ran his palm over its surface.

'What on earth *is* it?' he said. His voice sounded strange, as if he had a lump of something in his throat.

'I don't know. Something . . . ?'

'Something what?'

'Something from an Egyptian tomb or . . . ' Brin had seen hundreds of strange objects from other civilizations on all of her many museum visits. But she had never seen anything quite like this. 'Something from another civilization. Or something from another . . . ' she shook her head. 'I don't know.'

'How did it get here then?'

'I don't know that either.'

'Let's lift it away from the wall,' Chris whispered. 'We can get a better look.'

'We might damage it.'

'No . . . I don't think we will.' Chris tapped the surface with his fingernail. The sound seemed to echo round the tower like a melody.

They gently lifted the egg and carried it nearer the window. It was huge, too big to get their arms around and heavy . . . as much as they could do to lift it between them. Carefully, they laid it down.

By the light from the broken window they could see something on the side. There were three lines of strange, raised symbols. Symbols they had seen before.

$$\ni \supseteq \varkappa \Pi \varnothing \nu \lambda \kappa \nabla \subset \varnothing \varkappa \varkappa \varnothing \nu \nabla$$
$$\mathfrak{C} \nabla \mu \mathsf{C} / \Pi \supseteq \Delta \lambda \iota \kappa \varnothing \Pi \nu \Delta \varnothing \mathfrak{C} \mu \Pi \kappa / \mathsf{C} \nu \supseteq \varkappa$$
$$/ \lambda \iota \varnothing \ni \Delta \nabla \varkappa \mu \lambda \Pi \iota \Delta \Pi \subset \mathfrak{C} \varnothing / \iota \mathfrak{C} \lambda \kappa \nabla$$

Brin ran her fingers over them like a blind person reading braille. She felt them move beneath her gentle touch.

'They're like keys,' she said, her voice full of wonder.

'Keys . . . ?'

'Yes . . . keys on a keyboard.' She looked at him, her eyes shining. 'Keys, Chris . . . THE key!' She gripped his arm.

'Of course,' he exclaimed, realization dawning in his eyes. 'Where is it? Where's Tom's key—the one he drew from his dream?'

'It's under my bed . . . in that old case.'

'Shall I go and get it?'

Brin turned to him and smiled. 'Do you mind?'

Chris shook his head. He wasn't looking at her. His eyes were fixed on the egg.

He scrambled to his feet and was gone in a flash. Brin heard him clattering down the rickety stairs.

Brin sat cross-legged amid the dust and dirt of the mill-tower floor. Just looking. Motionless, as if the egg had cast a spell on her. When she brushed her hair from her eyes, she found her hand was shaking.

In no time at all Chris came belting back up the stairs. In his hand he held the two drawings of the key. The one Tom had done after his first dream and the one they had found in the old pram.

'Now we've got to be careful,' he said. They had a piece of paper each. 'If we press the wrong keys something awful might happen.'

'You go first,' Brin said, 'Do the top line.'

With efficiency that surprised her, Chris selected the symbols from the top line of Tom's drawing and punched them in.

$$\exists \nu \varnothing \varkappa \varkappa \varnothing$$

Then it was Brin's turn.

$$\nabla C / \supseteq \iota \varkappa \Delta \Pi \varnothing C \nu$$

Then Chris again.

$$\exists \varkappa \mu \Delta \varnothing \Phi \lambda$$

They sat, still as stone, waiting.

Nothing happened.

'Maybe there should be an "enter" key,' Chris whispered.

But they didn't need an 'enter' key. As they spoke the egg began to glow. It became the colour of moonlight, sparkling and shimmering as if lit by a thousand lamps. Then slowly a dark line appeared round the middle, thin, like a single hair at first. Then growing wider and wider. Gradually Brin realized the top half of the egg was opening. Then it stopped.

She heard Chris's breath come out like a gust of wind.

She took her hand away from her mouth.

'Chris . . . ?' She put her fingers out to seek his and felt them grasped and held, tight.

Then, like a flash of lightning, there was a kind of singing noise and a beam of silver light shot suddenly from the gap. They both gasped and sprung back as if they'd been shot. They landed in a heap together on the floor.

'Oh, my God,' Chris said. 'Look . . . !'

10

Chris—The Secret of the Egg

When they regained their balance, Chris and Brin realized what the beam was. On the floor in front of them a projected image began to appear.

'It's a hologram,' Chris whispered, 'a three-dimension—'

'I know what a hologram is,' Brin hissed. Then, touching his arm she said, her voice full of wonder, 'It's her, Chris . . . it's her.'

The hologram gradually took shape in front of them. A figure, a winged creature, slowly uncurling, stretching . . . the Snowbird . . .

Fully uncurled, she lifted her head, gazing towards them with huge, unblinking eyes that seemed almost to stare right through them and out, longingly, towards the light from the window. She moved her head to and fro, her long neck weaving from side to side. Slowly, she stood up. She stretched her frail arms above her head, fingers spread. Gradually, huge wings unfurled behind her. She flapped them once then folded them back against her body. She ran her hands through the crest of moonlight hair on her head then sat again, cross-legged on the floor, looking at them. The lower tips of her wings draped behind her like a bridal train.

Chris and Brin gazed at the Snowbird, starstruck. When she had been standing up, Chris reckoned she was about as tall as Brin's sister, Toni. Pale, bluish skin . . . her delicate body, fragile arms, legs . . . almost, but not quite, like a human being. She was gazing at them expectantly, a world of sadness and longing in her wide, ice-blue eyes.

Chris heard Brin whisper. It was as if her voice was coming from another world. She was shaking her head in disbelief.

'Chris, she's gorgeous. What *is* she? Where does she *come* from?'

'I don't believe this,' Chris gulped. 'I think I must be having one of Tom's dreams.' With difficulty he spoke again. Something seemed to be blocking up his throat. 'I don't know what she is,' he shook his head, ' . . . and I certainly don't know where she comes from.'

As he said it, the image began to fade. Then it disappeared altogether. Chris heard a little cry from Brin as if she couldn't bear to let the Snowbird go.

A new picture began to appear. A snowscape. There were mountains. Endless kilometres of white. Rising up from snowbound flatlands was a city of castles. Spire-lights twinkled like diamonds against a vast black sky. Flying machines ferried silently to and fro, spinning and rotating, their lights blurring blue, then silver, then gold, as they hovered over the city then sunk slowly out of sight.

'It's Tom's dreamscape,' Brin whispered.

'Do you think it's her home . . . where she comes from?' Chris shook his head in disbelief. 'It looks like . . . like another planet . . . '

'But how on earth did she get *here*?'

Suddenly, strange sounds began to come from the half open egg. A whistle, a few high notes. They merged into a kind of melody. Then came voices speaking strange languages. Gradually, a single voice emerged from the babble. It became clearer and clearer until they could understand what it said.

'Explorer Vessel *Ice Voyager* ZD 6874210 After being attacked by alien warships, explorer vessel *Ice Voyager* was marooned in an uncharted galaxy at an unknown time in its history. During the battle Crewmember SHANNAH was fatally injured. While the damaged space-time continuum converter was being repaired, a suitably climatic world was found for Crewmember Shannah to rest before her final flight. After the prescribed period of observation it was considered safe to leave Crewmember Shannah on an ice-bound island continent in the northern hemisphere of a tiny world in a nine-planet system. The capsule was sealed with her key and her personal hologram deposited into its memory banks.'

There was a click and a hiss and the voice faded. The beam grew stronger. Chris could see dust motes dancing like mosquitoes in the bright light. Shannah's image appeared again. Not life-size this time. Smaller, like watching a film. At first she was lying, curled round, apparently asleep. Then, gradually, she awoke. She spread her wings and took to the air. She circled, the now familiar sad-song echoing around the tower. As the image came close, Chris could see tears falling from her huge eyes. Her song faded until it became one long whisper of despair. The image dissolved and disappeared.

Out of the corner of his vision, Chris saw Brin shake her head and run her hand through her hair.

Again the image of Shannah's snow-bound homeland began to appear. As it did so a sharp, cold draught blew across Chris's face, sending fingers of ice through his hair. Then, all at once, the air was full of snowy-winged creatures. They flew in a 'V' formation. Four at the front carried a huge, silver-grey egg between them. They flew down and deposited it in the snow then, in a single formation, flew away. Time passed. A gradual darkening of the sky towards the left of the image. Then brightness grew from the right hand side. This happened several times until darkness and light seemed to merge into one. Then there came a beating of the air and a golden-winged creature appeared at the top of the circle of light. It soared round several times then came in to land beside the egg. It bent down and pressed a sequence of buttons on the side of the egg. Slowly it opened. Shannah emerged. Together, arms entwined, they circled. Shannah seemed to be taking a last look landward. They flew away together, across the city of castles, then away into the silver, snowlit distances. The egg crumpled, disintegrated, and disappeared into a white dust that merged with the snow.

Soon it seemed as if nothing had ever been there at all.

'Chris,' Brin whispered after a silence that seemed filled with sadness. 'It looked like . . . ?'

'What?'

'Like some kind of ceremony, a funeral.'

'A funeral?'

'Yes. I think it was supposed to show us Shannah's final flight.'

'What?'

'Final flight . . . the voice said Shannah was resting before her final flight, remember?'

'That's right, it did.'

Brin shook her head in bewilderment. 'What's it all supposed to mean, Chris?'

Chris frowned. 'I think . . . ?'

'What?'

'I think maybe they're trying to tell us they've left her in the wrong place. They thought the Fens during a long, snowy winter was a place the same as their own world . . . a place where they could leave her in preparation for her final flight.'

'You mean they didn't realize the season would change?'

'How could they? They had no information about Earth. They were lost, remember? Their space-time what-ever-it-was, was broken. They *thought* they stayed long enough to see what the climate was like and decided it was OK to leave her here.'

'And they didn't have a clue how far in time, or space, they'd travelled. Chris, do you realize they could have come from the future?'

Chris frowned. The thought that a space vessel from some time in the future could have landed in the Fenlands almost made him feel dizzy. It was the kind of thing that only happened in movies and in books . . . didn't it?

'They could have done, I suppose,' he said. 'Their technology looks pretty advanced.'

'Wow!' Brin said. 'Poor thing. She must hate it here. No wonder her sadness haunts the place. I wonder how long she's been here?'

'Ask.'

After a minute's thought Brin said, 'OK.' Chris heard her draw a deep breath. 'Shannah,' she whispered. Then, louder, gaining courage. 'Shannah? How long have you been here?'

There was a hiss and a whistle. Then the voice came again.

'Crewmember Shannah has been resting one hundred and ninety-five orbits round the fireplanet.'

'Fireplanet . . . ?'

'Sun . . . stupid,' Chris hissed.

'A hundred and ninety-five years . . . crikey . . . that would mean they left her here in . . . ?'

Chris frowned. 'I can't work it out in my head.'

'Neither can I . . . '

The voice came again.

'Crewmember Shannah must make her last flight before the fireplanet grows stronger again. She has rested too long . . . '

'Why?' Chris asked. 'Why has she rested too long?'

'Her body can no longer stand the temperature changes,' the voice explained. 'If she does not take her final flight to winterlands soon, her body will die. She must make her last flight or her spirit will never be free. There is no one here to guide her, that is why she asks for your help.'

The holo-beam divided in two and Shannah's image re-appeared. Her mouth opened but no sound emerged. She stood up on tiptoe and spread her wings. She stretched out her arms, pointing in one direction, then another and shaking her head in confusion. The holo-beams expanded, joined. They became almost the width of the tower room. The landscape-image became sharper. Snow began to fall. Shannah flapped her wings once. From her lips the sad-song came. Then the crest on her head grew dull and flat. She sank to the floor, wings folded around her like a shroud. The images faded. There was a click from the capsule. The beam faded then withdrew into silence.

'Wow!' Brin whispered at last. Then, 'Chris, look . . . !'

The egg-capsule began to hum. The lid began to open wider. With an almost inaudible hiss it stopped, fully open.

'Let's . . . ' Brin whispered.

They crept forward together.

Curled up inside, wings covering her body, eyes closed, was *Ice Voyager* Crewmember Shannah.

Chris stood frozen. It was stupid but he felt like crying. Beside him he heard a small noise come from from Brin's throat. He knelt down in front of the egg. Brin knelt beside him. When he looked at her she had tears in her eyes.

Chris stretched out his hand.

'I don't know if we should touch her.'

'It'll be OK. I'm sure she doesn't mean us any harm.' Tentatively he stroked the silken feathers. He almost expected his hand to go right through the curled-up body. It didn't.

Shannah was warm.

Alive!

'She looks so beautiful,' Brin whispered. 'I can't believe she's been dead all this time.'

'She's not dead.'

'What?' Brin looked at Chris in amazement.

'Feel,' Chris said.

Brin stroked Shannah softly with her fingertips.

'She's definitely not dead,' Chris murmured. 'Not as we know death anyway. She can't be, can she?'

'No.'

'Because she's got to make her last flight.'

'And we must help her,' Brin said, 'before it's too late. That's what she wants us to do. She doesn't know which way to go to find her last resting place.'

Chris said, 'She needs to go north to the Arctic, to where the voice called winterland. And somehow we've got to show her.'

As he spoke, the lid began to lower.

With a hiss the egg sealed itself shut.

Back indoors, still stunned, Chris stood staring out of Brin's bedroom window. His hands were thrust in the pockets of his jeans. He looked thoughtful. 'I don't know what we can do, Brin. We can hardly take her to the Arctic ourselves, can we?'

Brin didn't answer.

'I said we can't take her to the . . . ?' Chris turned.

'I heard you, Chris. I was just thinking how gorgeous she was. How sad. Curled up like that. I wanted to look at her for ever.'

'You know, the more I think about it, the more I'm sure Mrs Mirston and her husband knew she was there.'

'What . . . you mean they actually found the egg?'

'I'm not sure. But I think she tried to tell them through dreams. Like Tom. But they never understood. I think maybe your aunt had got so used to seeing her she talked to her all the time. I mean . . . ' he hesitated. 'I know she was old, and ill, but there was something really weird about the way she went around as if someone was with her all the time. Like one of those imaginary friends kids have . . . you know.'

'Yes, Toni used to have one. His name was Margaret.'

'*His* name was Margaret?'

'Yep. She insisted it was a boy called Margaret.'

'She's a bit weird, your sister.'

'Is she? Yes . . . I suppose she is.' Brin looked at the painting on her lap. 'And you know, Chris,' she went on, 'I'm totally sure Uncle Jacob *must* have actually seen Shannah too. This is so exactly like her. And he must have seen the symbols or else how could he have known what to write underneath.'

'Tom drew the symbols from his dream, remember. Shannah could have used your uncle in the same way she's used Tom—it's just that no one understood.'

'I don't suppose we'll ever know,' Brin said sadly.

'No.'

'I bet they thought she was a ghost, same as we did.'

'I didn't really ever think that.'

'Neither did I.'

Brin and Chris looked at each other and smiled.

'I wonder how it could speak our language?' Chris said.

'Probably through hearing voices all those years . . . how long did they say?'

'A hundred and ninety-five years.'

'That would be . . . ' Brin handed Chris the painting and took a pencil and paper from her desk. 'Umm . . . 1799 . . . ' she frowned. 'That's funny.'

'What?'

'I was reading something . . . I know.' Brin got off the bed and dashed downstairs. She ran back up, two at a time. In her hand she held the book of Fenland tales. She flicked through it quickly. Finding the page she wanted, she scanned the text. She turned to Chris, her eyes shining. 'I don't believe it!'

'What?' Chris didn't know if he wanted any more surprises. The first one hadn't really sunk in yet.

'Listen . . . "during the harsh winter of 1799 a woman named Elizabeth Woodcock survived being trapped in the snow for eight days. She fell off her horse when it was scared by a meteor that flashed through the black, snow-laden sky" . . . ' Brin looked up at Chris.

'Yeah . . . so?'

'So perhaps it wasn't a meteor, perhaps it was *Ice Voyager* bringing Shannah . . . '

'Come off it, Brin.'

'Or maybe it was a shuttle craft or something.'

'Brin, we don't *know* that, do we?'

'But Chris . . . look, it all fits. A very harsh winter . . . ' she turned back a page. 'Look at this . . . '

There was an illustration. A picture of a frozen Fenland landscape with the spires of Ely Cathedral rising up from the snow like a city of castles.

'It looks just like . . . ' Chris looked up. 'Wow!' he said.

'That's right. It does . . . and listen . . . ' Brin read on excitedly. ' "*The Cambridgeshire Independent Press and Chronicle* reported many tragedies resulting from the severe weather . . . " ' She looked up. 'Oh, Chris, there was another tragedy they didn't know about . . . poor Shannah marooned here in a climate she hates. Waiting for her last flight but not knowing in which direction to go. Chris, what are we going to do?'

Chris was afraid she'd start crying. He hated it when women cried. Worse thing was, he still felt like crying himself. Who in the world would have thought that hidden in the old mill-tower was a creature from another planet? The whole thing was just bonkers.

'What I don't understand is . . . ' Brin was saying, 'if she's been here for all this time, why hasn't anyone but my aunt and uncle seen her before?'

Chris shrugged. He wished Brin wouldn't keep asking him things. 'I dunno,' he said. 'Maybe she only comes out in winter, when it's really cold . . . when there's hardly anyone about.'

'But she was in that photo. It was taken during the summer.'

'That's true.'

'There aren't any stories about ghostly birds or anything in my mum's book.'

'No.'

'You'd think *someone* would have seen her though, wouldn't you?'

'Well, if they have they've kept it to themselves. Mr and Mrs Mirston certainly did.'

Suddenly Chris needed to be alone. He needed to think. He looked at his watch. 'I've got to go,' he said. 'My dad'll have a fit if I'm late.'

Brin sat cross-legged on the bed, the book on her lap.

'But . . . '

'Look, Brin . . . I've got to think this out. I need to concentrate.'

'But . . . ?'

'You try and think of something too, OK?'

Brin nodded. 'Barring an expedition to the Arctic I don't know what . . . ?'

'We'll work something out—we've got to. We can't just abandon her.'

'Chris, I still don't know if it was really her we saw by the river that evening . . . or if it was her ghost.'

'Can you have a ghost from the future do you think?'

'I don't even know if you can have a ghost from the past.'

'I think probably she's just so unhappy,' Chris said, 'that she kind of . . . creates an image with her mind. And that's what we saw and what she made Tom see in his dreams.'

'Perhaps that's what ghosts are anyway, projections of unhappiness.'

'Yes,' Chris looked thoughtful. 'Yes . . . perhaps they are.'

'But we found her feathers,' Brin said, picking one up and stroking it softly. 'So she must really come out sometimes.'

'Yes,' Chris said.

Later, when Chris had had time to think, when he had been sitting on his bed for what seemed like hours and the solution had suddenly come to him like a snowball from the blue, he phoned Brin.

Her mother answered.

'I'll just get her, Chris,' she said. Chris heard her call up the stairs. 'Brin . . . it's for you-hoo!'

Then he heard Brin say, 'He must be psychic, I was just going to phone him.'

'Brin,' he said excitedly, 'I've worked it out.'

'Oh, Chris,' she said, laughing. 'So have I!'

11

Brin—Shannah in Danger

Brin thought, that first, incredible winter at Dimmocks, that the snow would never, ever melt. It was wonderful at first but after weeks of tramping through muddy slush to the bus-stop, plus getting laughed at for wearing green wellies to school, the novelty most definitely wore off. And after having chilblains and one horrendous burst hot water bottle in her bed, Brin, at least, was ready to see the back of it.

She and Chris couldn't wait for the thaw to set in. For it was then they planned to rescue the Snowbird.

Brin didn't know how they managed to keep the discovery to themselves. They were both absolutely bursting to tell somebody. But, if by any chance someone happened to actually believe them, who knew what would happen to the Snowbird? They knew that people did awful experiments on animals and they could both imagine what they might do to one from another world. They decided it was definitely their secret. And the sooner they rescued Shannah, the better.

The trouble was Brin felt sure Toni had guessed something was going on.

'Why do you and Chris always talk secretly?' she'd asked. 'Is he your boyfriend or something?'

'Don't be stupid, Toni,' Brin had said. 'Anyway, we don't.'

'Yes, you do. You're planning something, I know. Why can't he be my friend too.'

'He *is* your friend. He's been out biking with you, hasn't he?'

'Once,' Toni had said sulkily.

'Well, he's busy. He has to help his dad. And he's looking after a swan that flew into the power lines. He said you could go up and see it didn't he?'

'When?'

Brin had shrugged, glad she'd been able to change the subject. 'Whenever you like.'

'OK, I'll go tomorrow. Will he mind?'

'No, of course he won't, Toni. He said you could, didn't he?'

Brin almost told Toni then. She knew her sister was lonely at Dimmocks. That she still missed her London friends and was finding it hard to make new ones. But, deep down, Brin knew it would be stupid to even hint that something was going on. And even if Toni believed her, which was doubtful, Toni couldn't keep a secret if her life depended on it.

Almost every evening Brin crept up the old mill stairs to make sure the egg was still there. She had horrible visions of her father discovering it while she was at school. Or the floor suddenly collapsing, sending it smashing to the room below. Brin would take her torch and when the silver-grey egg caught the light from its beam like a bright star peeping out, she would heave a sigh of relief. She would sit, cross-legged, in front of the stack of timber, telling Shannah of their plans. She didn't know if Shannah heard her or not but she told her anyway. If anyone had seen her, Brin thought they would be convinced she had gone off her head. Talking to herself. Except Great-Aunt Winnie, or her husband, the unsuitable and mysterious Uncle Jacob. Brin felt sure they would have known what she was doing. There was no doubt about it. They *had* known about Shannah. But whether they had actually discovered the egg and managed to open it, or had just seen visions of the Snowbird on misty and mysterious fenland evenings, she and Chris would never know.

As time went on, Brin felt herself becoming more and more curious about her aunt and uncle. Some day, she promised herself, when the adventure with Shannah was over, she would find out about their lives. After all, someone must know. Most of all she wanted to know why her aunt's family had disliked her husband so much. Brin felt that anyone who could paint such gorgeous pictures must have been a really nice person.

Then, one day, something awful happened.

It was getting towards the middle of February. It was still bitterly cold. The ice and snow still refused to melt and the land was still clutched in its grip of iron. The most prolonged spell of below freezing temperatures for a hundred years, the weathermen said. Chris and Brin had begun to think it would be too late to rescue Shannah. They knew she would not survive another summer.

That day, Mrs Carter picked them up from the bus-stop.

'Weather forecast's good,' she said. 'Thaw setting in at last.'

Brin hadn't realized, until they came to live at Dimmocks, what it was like to have your lives ruled by the weather.

'And your dad saw Ben Smith this morning,' Anne Carter added cheerfully. 'He said the ice is melting along Wicken Lode. Soon be spring.'

Brin felt her heart thud with excitement. She saw Chris glance at her in the rear view mirror. She grinned and gave him a thumbs up sign.

When she got home there was a Toyota pick-up truck in the driveway. The door to the mill-tower was open. Voices came from inside. She peeped in.

'Dad, I'm home.'

Her father and a man with a beard were kneeling on the floor studying something.

David looked up and grinned. 'This is Mr Gibbs,' he said. 'He's going to do some work for us.'

Brin saw they were studying plans and drawings of some kind. She recognized a sketch of the outside of the tower.

'What are you going to do?' she asked, suddenly scared.

'Do up the old place, make an office upstairs for your dad's computers.'

'What . . . soon?' Brin's voice must have sounded a bit cranky because they both looked at her in surprise.

'Yes, Brin, you knew I intended to use it as an office,' her father said. 'That spare room's much too small. I need more space if I'm going to have all the hardware I need.'

'Yes, but I thought you were going to do it yourself . . . next year or something?'

98

'Well, I was, but we decided to get a builder to do it. There's so much else to do and I've only got one pair of hands. It doesn't matter, does it?'

'Er . . . ' Brin swallowed. 'No, of course not. When . . . ?'

But they had gone back to the plans. Mr Gibbs was waving his arms about and saying something about clearing the top floor. Then he was going on about load-bearing beams and stuff. Brin's imagination began to run away with her. She saw the builders finding Shannah. Telling everyone. What a stink the whole thing would cause. The egg being carted off to some horrible scientific research laboratory . . .

Brin pulled on her father's sleeve. 'Dad . . . when will they start?'

'Should start next week, love,' Mr Gibbs said. 'Weather'll be better then. With a bit of luck.'

Panic stricken, Brin rushed indoors and rang Chris.

'He's out in the workshop,' Mrs Carter said. 'Working on that old pram of your aunt's. Can I give him a message?'

'Please ask him to ring me. It's important.'

'Something to do with homework is it?'

'No—something *really* important.'

Brin heard Mrs Carter laugh. 'All right, dear.'

Brin could tell by her voice what kind of smile she had on her face. In fact, both parents thought their friendship quite amusing for reasons Brin couldn't make out. For instance, when she asked if Chris could repair Aunt Winnie's old pram, her father had grinned and said, 'What's he want to do that for, Brin? You two planning on . . . ?' He'd waved his hands in the air and raised his eyebrows in an aggravating way. Brin thought parents could be really stupid at times.

'Give me a break, Dad,' Brin had said. 'We just thought it might be fun, that's all. Chris thought he could make a go-kart or something out of it.'

Brin hated telling lies, especially to people she loved. But there were times when you absolutely had to.

When Chris phoned back she blurted it all out in a rush. He had to tell her to calm down. That was one thing about Chris, he never panicked.

'Chris, what can we *do*?'

'We'll have to move her.'

'Where to?'

'I dunno.'

'I'm really scared. Chris, we must do something.'

'We only need a week or two more.'

'But it'll be too late. The builders are supposed to be starting next week!'

'My dad says builders never start work when they say they are going to.'

'I hope he's right, Chris.' Brin didn't think she could bear it if anything happened to Shannah now. Not when she had been waiting for so long.

Mrs Carter had been right. The very next day the sun came out and the snow began to melt. And when the sun came out, Brin developed the worst cold in the history of the world.

'You've got a bit of a temperature,' her father said, holding his hand to her forehead. 'You'd better stay home from school.'

'Oh, Dad . . . ?' Brin thought she managed to sound quite convincing.

'But you'll stay in bed, OK?' he said sternly.

She snuggled under the duvet. 'OK, Dad.' Brin sniffed, coughed. Then sneezed for good measure.

Two days and half a dozen Lem-sips later, Brin was bored. She put on her tracksuit bottoms and a thick jumper and went downstairs.

'Can I watch telly?' she asked, putting her head round the door. Her father was busy at his computer. He swivelled round on his chair.

'If you make me a cup of tea.'

'It's a deal,' Brin said.

'Oh,' he called, 'and make one for Darren will you?'

'Who's Darren?'

'He works for Rod Gibbs, he's started clearing out the tower-loft.'

Brin went cold, as if a splinter of ice had entered her heart. The top of her head went numb as if someone had sliced a bit off. She thought it just showed you could never believe what adults say. Not only did the builders plan to start when they promised. They'd come a week *early*.

Brin had never made a cup of tea so quickly in all her life.

As soon as she went outside she knew something terrible was happening. There was a pile of junk on the ground outside the tower. Old newspapers, sacks, wooden boxes. Most of it had been thrown from the top window. And, horror of horrors, Brin recognized the planks of timber that had been stacked in front of the egg. As she stood there, a black polythene sack full of something came sailing from the window and landed a metre or two away from her astonished feet.

She pushed open the door and hurried up the stairs as fast as she was able without spilling too much tea.

A youth in grubby denim dungarees and a red baseball cap was bending over something against the wall. Brin knew straight away what it was. Horror froze her to the spot. Brin saw the youth take a hammer and screwdriver from his tool-bag. She lunged forward, spilling hot tea over the back of her hand. But she was too late. The youth put the screwdriver against the egg and banged it with the hammer. Hard. The wild, metallic ringing echoed round the tower. Brin put a hand over her ear. Darren dropped the hammer as if he'd been burned. The screwdriver skittered across the floor towards her. When Brin looked, she saw the end was bent and twisted as if it had been struck by lightning. Even when she took her hand away, her eardrum was still ringing.

'Darren!' she shouted. 'I've brought your tea.' She saw him jump then turn round in surprise.

'Jeez,' he said. He wiggled the hand that had held the hammer. He blew on his fingers then stuck them under his armpit. 'Where'd you come from?'

'I came up the stairs,' Brin said stupidly.

She handed him the tea. 'I'm afraid I spilt some.' She rubbed the back of her hand on her tracksuit trousers.

'Ta.' Darren took a noisy mouthful. He indicated the egg. 'Got any idea what that is? Found it behind that stack of old timber. Gov'nor said to let him know if I found anything valuable. I tried to open it.' He shook his hand again. 'I don't know what stuff it's made of.' He sniffed. 'Nearly broke me bleedin' 'and.'

Brin was surprised at the speed with which the idea came into her head.

'Oh,' she said casually. 'It's my brother's.' She tried not to sound as if her heart was right up in her mouth. 'He'll do his nut if you've damaged it. It's the latest toy, haven't you seen them? They're all the rage.'

Darren looked at her. He fingered his ear-ring thoughtfully. 'You 'avin' me on?'

'No, honestly. Ask him if you don't believe me.'

'What sort of toy is it then?' Darren still looked suspicious. He crouched down and touched the egg with his fingertips. 'Feels as if it's frez,' he said, ' . . . and what's this?' He poked his finger on one of the key symbols.

'It's supposed to be alien writing,' Brin said quickly. 'You know, something like hieroglyphics.'

'Like what?'

'Hieroglyphics . . . Egyptian writing . . . you know.'

Darren looked at her as if he didn't have a clue what she was on about. He stood up. 'So,' he said. 'What's it supposed to be, then?'

'It's a space station. It opens up in the middle but Tom's the only one with the key.' Brin was telling fibs as if she had done it all her life. 'You . . . er, have to punch a sequence of symbols then it opens . . . you know . . . like the combination of a safe.'

Darren screwed up his nose. 'What's it doing up 'ere then?' Darren rolled the egg towards the window to get a better look. It veered off sideways and Darren kicked it straight with the toe of his D.M.

Brin winced. She thought about trying to stop him but realized that any strange behaviour would arouse his suspicions even more.

'He hides it from my sister. He won't let anyone else play with it.' She grinned. 'You know what six year olds are like.'

'Yeah,' he said. ' 'Orrible. Brought it up 'ere on his own then, did he?' Darren said suspiciously. 'Feels pretty heavy to me. Too big for a kid's toy.'

'Er . . . I helped him. He had it for Christmas, I'm sure if you look in the toy sho—'

Just then Brin heard a vehicle pull into the drive. She looked out of the window. 'Here's Mr Gibbs,' she said. She tried to disguise the anxiety in her voice. If *he* came up and saw the egg he'd never believe it was a kid's toy. Darren might be a bit thick, but Mr Gibbs certainly wasn't.

Brin saw her father come out of the house and speak to him. They both looked up at the window. Mr Gibbs waved. 'Tell Darren I'd like a word,' he shouted.

Darren went over and stood beside her. 'Bet 'e's come to check up on me,' he said in a disgruntled voice. 'Miserable sod.'

'Er . . . Darren,' Brin said, 'please don't tell anyone about the space station.'

'Why's that then?' Brin didn't really think he had believed a word she'd said. Perhaps she wasn't very good at telling lies after all?

'Well, my parents get annoyed when Tom won't share his things. And he's not really supposed to come in here in case he hurts himself. He'll get into a row. Please . . . '

'I dunno,' Darren said. 'I know what you flipping kids are. I still dunno if you're telling me—'

Brin tried to look innocent and sweet. Quite a hard thing for her to do. 'Oh, go on, Darren,' she said. 'Don't be a pig.'

Darren looked at her for a minute, frowning. Eventually he said, 'Come on, then, let's get it downstairs. The electricians are coming tomorrow.'

'I don't know if Tom would like us to . . . '

'My orders is to clear the place out,' Darren said obstinately. 'I'll get the gov'nor to give me a hand if you—'

'No,' Brin said loudly. Too loudly. Darren gave her an odd look. 'I'll give you a hand. It's not that heavy, honestly. We can easily carry it between us.'

'Will it go in one of these sacks?' Darren held up a black polythene rubbish bag. He grinned. 'We could chuck it out of the winder.' Brin could see he was having her on.

'You're joking!' she exclaimed. 'It cost a fortune.'

Darren's D.Ms clumped down the rickety stairs to the floor below. Luckily, David and Mr Gibbs were still outside.

'Let's put it in there,' she said, nodding her head towards the cupboard under the stairs. 'Tom would hate Toni to find it.'

'Little so and so,' Darren remarked.

'Thanks for helping me. I'll just make sure the door's shut properly.'

When she got outside, Darren was saying something to Mr Gibbs. When she appeared they stopped talking. They looked at her. With a sudden stab of fear Brin knew that Shannah was in more danger now than she had ever been before. They had to get her out that very night.

Or else it could well be too late!

12

Chris—The Old Boathouse

When Chris got home from school there was an urgent message from Brin.

'I thought she was sick,' he said.

'She still sounded as if she'd got a cold,' Mrs Carter told him. 'Anyway, she wants you to ring her.'

What now, Chris thought? They'd made all their plans. All they'd got to do was wait a few more days and everything would be OK.

'Chris, something awful's happened.' He could tell by Brin's voice that she wasn't joking.

'What?'

Brin told him what had happened.

'It looks as if we'd better get her out tonight, then.'

'Yes, but where can we take her?'

Chris thought a minute. 'What about the old boathouse? She should be safe there until—'

'Chris, it's falling to bits. Dad's going to knock it down when he's got time.'

'You tell me where else, then? We'll never get it to Highfen without someone seeing.'

He heard Brin sigh. 'I suppose it'll have to be the boathouse then. Can you bike over later?'

When Chris told his mother he was going to cycle along to Dimmocks she said, 'Come with me and Marjorie if you like. You can put your bike in the back of the Land Rover to ride home. I've promised to drop some eggs in on the way to the WI meeting.'

When they arrived, Alex blew the dust off a couple of chairs, apologized for the mess and invited everyone to sit down.

'There's a car parked just up the lane,' Anne Carter remarked. 'I thought you might have visitors.'

'Someone fishing, I expect,' Alex said. 'There's often cars parked in the lay-by.'

Chris saw Marjorie Smith glance through into the front room. There was a pile of rubble on the floor where Brin's father had been knocking brickwork out to expose the inglenook. Toni was sitting amongst it, watching television.

'All the years I've lived nearby,' Mrs Smith said, 'and I've never been inside this house.'

'I wish we could find out more about my aunt and uncle,' Brin said. She was sitting, red-nosed, at the table, reading *Lord of the Rings*.

David came downstairs with Tom wrapped in a bath towel. Tom was struggling, trying to dry Scott Tracy with the corner of it. His father plonked him down in the chair by the Rayburn.

'Stay,' he commanded as if Tom was a dog. He went to the airing cupboard and took out a clean, unironed pair of pyjamas and threw them at him.

'That damn Rayburn's gone out again,' Alex remarked.

'I'll relight it in a minute,' David said. He rummaged in a pile of papers on the mantelpiece. 'Speaking of Aunt Winnie, I had a letter from the solicitor this morning . . . oh yes, here it is.' He passed it to Alex.

'We have in our possession various documents and papers belonging to Mrs Mirston . . . and . . . ' she read a few more lines of the letter to herself. Then she looked up. 'Are you going to say we'd like to have the documents, David?' she asked.

'Yes, of course,' David replied. 'Who knows what family secrets they might reveal?'

'There might be something about the locket,' Alex said to Chris's mother.

'There might.' Mrs Carter shook her head. 'But I've really come to the conclusion it must have fallen off somewhere. But where, is a mystery.'

Chris thought then that there were more mysteries about Dimmocks than Brin's parents, or his mother, or anyone in the world would ever have dreamed of.

'Can I show Chris the mill-loft now it's cleared out?' Brin asked suddenly. She took a tissue from the pocket of her jeans and blew her nose.

'What . . . in the dark?' her mother said.

Brin shrugged. 'We can take torches. I just thought I'd show him what the builders were doing.'

Her father looked dubious. 'Well, be careful of those stairs.' He struck a match to relight the Rayburn then put the box back on the mantelpiece.

'We will. Come on, Chris.'

'It's not fair,' Toni stood in the kitchen doorway. 'Why are *they* allowed in there and not me and Tom.'

'You know why,' David said.

Toni stamped her foot.

'If you're going to do that, you can go up to your room, young lady,' Alex said.

'All right then, I will!' Toni stormed off.

Outside, Chris said, 'We'd better wait until Mum's gone.'

'OK, let's just get the boathouse doors open ready.'

The boathouse was in a terrible state. The upper timbers were full of dry rot, one leg had collapsed. In fact the whole building hung at a precarious angle over the water.

Between them they managed to force one of the double doors open a metre or so. It was pitch dark inside, a smell of decay. Chris shone his torch. Its beam revealed crumbling timbers, a couple of old diesel cans and a pile of oily rags. There was a coil of decayed-looking rope on the platform. Below, the river lapped softly against the sides.

'I've been in here before,' Chris said. 'A friend of my dad's used to keep his motor boat in here. Before the leg collapsed,' he added. He shone his torch upwards. Slung between the rafters above their heads was an old wooden canoe.

'Boy,' Chris said. 'I didn't know that was there. We couldn't half have some fun with it.'

'It's probably falling to bits.'

'Looks OK.' He shone his torch around the rest of the building. 'The walls look a bit dodgy,' he said. 'But this platform looks all right.' He bent down. 'It's dry as a bone.'

'Chris, be careful.'

'Yep, it'll take the weight all right.'

'Chris, I'm not sure . . . '

'Brin, there's nowhere else. She'll be all right in here until—'

'OK, OK . . . '

Round the front, they heard the slamming of doors. The Land Rover started up. Alex called goodbye.

'Come on,' Chris said. 'The sooner we get her out, the better.'

Afterwards, Chris didn't know how they managed to get the egg out without anyone seeing. As they crept past the kitchen window they could see Brin's parents sitting at the table. Thomas was watching TV in the front room. Toni must still be up in her room, sulking.

Together, they lugged the egg across the lawn and down to the river. They rolled it carefully inside the boathouse and wedged it in a corner. Brin covered it with an old blanket she had found in a cupboard in the mill-tower. They pulled the door shut as quietly as they could.

'It's only for a day or two,' Chris said. 'I saw Ben today, the ice at Wicken has almost gone.'

'Thank goodness for that.'

Suddenly Chris clutched Brin's arm. 'Shh, a minute!'

'What?'

Chris shrugged. 'Nothing. I thought I heard voices,' he laughed. 'I must be imagining things.'

'It's the TV, stupid,' Brin laughed. 'Tom always has it up loud.'

Chris breathed a sigh of relief. He was getting a nervous wreck. There was no doubt about it, the sooner they got Shannah to safety, the better!

13

Brin—A Sad Ending?

Brin found it hard to sleep. Tossing and turning, images of Shannah were haunting her mind. What if they were too late? What would happen if, by the time they had carried out their plan, spring had come to the Fenland and Shannah would be lost for ever? Brin didn't think she could bear it if Shannah died before they managed to rescue her.

From the next room, she could hear Tom's bed creaking as he tossed and turned. No more nightmares had come to disturb him since she and Chris discovered the secret of the egg. Toni still complained about his tossing, his turning. She said the sound of his mumbled dreams kept her awake. Alex had given up the idea of taking him to the doctor. She decided it was just a stage Tom was going through. Brin knew that parents were always thinking their kids were going through stages of one kind or another. It was just that Thomas seemed to go through more than most.

Brin had peeped into their room before going to bed. Toni was still awake but had turned away from Brin's kiss goodnight.

'Don't sulk, Toni,' Brin had whispered. 'It's only because Dad doesn't want you to get hurt he won't let you go in the mill-tower.'

Toni had said something that sounded like 'pooh'.

Brin had sighed and straightened Tom's covers before tip-toeing out and shutting the door.

Outside, Brin heard the eerie hoot of an owl, the far distant and diminishing roar of a train. The cry of a vixen echoed from across the lonely fen. She shivered and drew her covers up to her chin.

The next thing she knew, she was wide awake again. It was still dark, a pale crescent moon shone in the gap between the curtains. She heard someone go stealthily downstairs.

Brin got out of bed and threw her old cardigan round her shoulders. She went along the corridor. Her parents' bedroom door was open.

'Mum . . . what's going on?'

Alex was sitting up in bed. 'Dad thought he heard someone outside.'

'Shall I go down?'

'No, stay here.' Alex got out of bed. At the top of the stairs she called out. 'David, you OK?'

Brin's father appeared in the hallway. 'Can't see anything,' he said, coming up. He looked puzzled. 'I swear I heard noises outside but there's no sign of anyone out there. Sorry, Brin, did I wake you up?'

'Did you take a good look round,' Alex asked anxiously.

'Yes . . . I went right out into the lane. It was probably those fishermen Marjorie and Anne saw. We'll have to get that dog I promised. Go back to bed, Brin, everything's OK.'

But it was ages before Brin dropped off again.

In the morning she awoke to see the sun rising, blood red, over the fen. She realized Tom was shouting from his room.

'Fire! Help! International Rescue!'

Brin groaned and turned over. Trust Tom to be having an adventure this time of the morning.

She suddenly became aware of running feet. Her door flew open.

'Brin . . . !' It was her mother. 'Quick, the boathouse is on fire!'

Dread lent wings to Brin's feet as she leapt out of bed. From her window she could see a cloud of evil black smoke rising from the bottom of the garden. Stricken with panic she flung on her cardigan and dashed downstairs.

Tom was in the kitchen doorway, jumping up and down with excitement. 'Brin! Brin! Look . . . '

As she lurched outside into the early morning, Brin thought that today was definitely going to be the worst day of her life. She could see her father running towards the river bank, his dressing gown flapping around him like the wings of a bat. Alex wasn't far behind, dressed in her overcoat and wellingtons. Brin hurtled after them, clutching Tom's hand as he ran by her side. Alex turned, her face white with fear.

'Brin,' she shouted. 'Where's Toni, have you seen Toni?'

Brin skidded to a halt. 'Toni!' She shook Tom's arm. 'Tom, is Toni still upstairs?'

Tom shook his head, pulling at Brin's arm. 'No, she wasn't there when I woke up . . . come on, I want to see!'

'Where *is* she, Tom?'

'I don't know . . . ' he pointed suddenly. 'There she is . . . ' Toni was standing behind one of the apple trees, peering round the trunk. 'Come *on*, Brin, I want to see the fire.'

'Mum, it's OK, she's here,' Brin shouted.

Alex came running up. She grabbed Toni and hugged her. 'Oh, Ant, we didn't know where you were.'

Brin noticed her sister was crying.

David was standing in front of the boathouse, watching helplessly as smoke and flames poured out from between the timbers.

'Dad, I've got to go in there!' Her heart wild with terror, Brin lunged forward. Her father caught the back of her cardigan.

'Brin, are you mad?'

She struggled as he held her arms. It was only afterwards she realized tears had been streaming down her cheeks. She put her hands over her face. 'Dad . . . I've got to . . . '

There was a crash and the flames leapt higher as the roof caved in. The river below hissed and boiled like a witch's cauldron.

'Brin, there's nothing in there.' David shook his head in dismay. 'It's a shame but I was going to pull it down anyway. There's no danger to the house so we may as well let it burn. God knows how it caught fire—' he broke off, shaking his head again. 'I knew I heard someone about last night, I should have called the police. Bloody vandals,' he added angrily. 'I thought we'd get away from all this when we left the city.'

He took off his dressing gown and put it round Brin's shoulders. 'Come on in, Brinna, we'll both freeze to death.'

Brin wrenched herself away. Ignoring her father's startled call, she ran back towards the house. Her breath came out in sobs. She ran upstairs and threw herself on the bed, crying as if her heart was broken.

'What am I going to tell Chris?' she sobbed. 'What am I going to tell Chris?'

Suddenly, Tom appeared in the doorway. He had trailed all the way upstairs in his muddy boots.

'What's up, Brin?' he asked.

Brin wiped the back of her hand across her eyes. 'Nothing,' she croaked.

Tom came to sit beside her. She turned her head away so he could not see the anguish on her face. She felt his little hand touch her shoulder.

'It's all right, Brin,' he said. 'You don't have to cry. It's only a silly old boathouse.'

Brin rubbed her face into the pillow. 'It's not that, Tom,' she sobbed again. 'You don't understand.'

'Yes, I do,' he said. He got up and went out of the room. Brin heard him running down the stairs, then up again laughing as if the end of the world hadn't come.

Through her misery, Brin heard the roar of an engine outside and a motor vehicle screech to a halt in front of the house.

A bit later, she heard her mother on the telephone, explaining why she'd be late for work. Then she came into Brin's room.

'You all right, Brin?' she sat on the bed and put her hand on Brin's shoulder. 'You should be getting ready for school.'

Brin buried her head further into the pillow and managed to croak, 'Yes.'

'John Carter came rushing over. He saw the smoke . . .'

Brin wiped her face and sat up. Her mother looked at her, puzzled. 'Is Chris with him?' Brin asked, sniffing.

Alex shook her head. 'No, he's gone off early, some school trip.'

'I don't know how I'm going to tell him,' Brin blurted out the words helplessly.

Alex frowned. 'What . . . about the boathouse? Why will Chris care?'

'Oh . . . there was an old canoe in there . . . he said we could take it on the river.'

Alex put her arm round Brin and gave her a hug. 'Never mind, Brin. It could have been much worse.'

But Brin knew that nothing in the whole world could have been worse.

'Toni did it,' she said later on the telephone to Chris. As she spoke, her eyes filled with tears. She brushed them away angrily. Crying wouldn't bring Shannah back. Nothing would.

Chris's voice was full of anger and pain. 'How did Toni do it, I don't understand?'

'She'd seen us go down there. She was watching us from her window apparently. Then, early this morning she went to see what we'd been up to.'

'But how did she set it on fire?'

'She couldn't find the torch so she took Dad's matches. She must have dropped one on those old rags and stuff . . . oh, Chris, poor Shannah. I'm really sorry.'

Brin could hear a strange break in Chris's voice. 'It's not your fault, Brin . . . '

'But I should have realized Toni might be watching.'

'How could you?'

Brin sighed. 'I know what she's like, that's how. Perhaps if I'd told her about Shannah . . . ?'

'No,' Chris said quickly. 'She'd have let on. I know she would. What did your mum and dad say? Did she get a wallop?'

'No, they hardly ever smack us. Mum says Toni was so scared when she saw what she had done, she's been punished enough. And it'll stop her playing with matches for ever.'

She heard Chris sigh. 'Did they ask you why we'd been down there?'

'Yes. I had to tell a lie . . . I said we were just looking around.'

'Have you been down there . . . there's no hope that . . . ?'

'No,' Brin said tearfully. 'There's nothing left. Only a pile of smouldering timbers . . . nothing.'

Early that evening, Tom called Brin into the front room.

'Look what I done at school today, Brin.' He pulled a screwed up piece of paper from his Thunderbirds lunchbox.

'Well, at least you did something,' she said, miserably, remembering how she had sat all day gazing out of the window and thinking of the Snowbird. She took the drawing from him. She frowned. Her brother was looking at her expectantly. 'What's this, Tom?'

'It's a egg.'

'An Easter egg—honestly, Tom, we've only just had Christmas.'

Tom made a face. 'No, silly, a egg in a nest.'

'Have you been doing nature at school today?'

Tom shook his head. 'No, I dreamed it during arithmetic.'

Brin's eyes flew open wide. She felt her heart thud a wild beat of hope. 'A dream, Tom? Like those others you used to have.'

'No, I was awake, silly. Anyway, this was a happy dream.' He took the painting from Brin's hand. 'See . . . ' he pointed to a round shape with letters in blue and pink crayon on the side. 'This is a egg . . . this is a nest.' There was a pile of what looked like twigs and grass beside a sign of some kind. There was writing on the sign, letters jumbled up.

'It's a jolly big egg,' Brin said carefully. 'How big is it, Tom?'

Tom shrugged. 'Dunno.'

'Where is it then, where is the nest?'

He shrugged again. 'Dunno.'

Later, when Chris arrived, Brin showed him the picture. He stared at it for a long time, frowning. Then his eyes lit up. 'I know where it is,' he said, his voice full of suppressed excitement. 'It's just down the lane. Look, that's the sign that says "Upware" only Tom's put the "p" and the "e" the wrong way round.'

'He's always doing that,' Brin said. 'You know, he passes that sign every day on the way to school, but he says he dreamt it.'

Chris looked at her. 'Do you think . . . ?'

Brin shook her head, sorrowfully. 'It was just a dream, Chris. Shannah's dead. How could she . . . ?' Her eyes filled with tears.

Chris got up suddenly. 'Well, I'm going to look!' He wrenched his coat from the back of the chair.

Brin hurried after him. 'Wait, Chris . . . I'm coming too.'

There was a car parked down the road. Two figures stood by the roadside. Even in the twilight, Brin knew who one of them was.

Chris and Brin ran towards them. Brin's heart was beating so loudly she thought everyone could hear.

Chris skidded to a halt. He put his hand on Brin's arm. 'It's Darren Smart and his brother,' he hissed. 'What on earth are they doing? What's Darren got . . . ?'

The two figures turned in surprise as Chris and Brin arrived. Darren looked guiltily down at the old blanket he held in his hand. He hurriedly threw it into the hedge.

'What you doing here?' Darren narrowed his eyes suspiciously.

'What are *you* doing here, Darren?' Brin said. 'Surely you finished work ages ago?' As she spoke, her eyes caught something gleaming in the hedge. Chris must have heard her sharp intake of breath. He looked at her. Suddenly afraid, she shook her head and frowned at him furiously. She bent down and picked up the blanket. 'Where did you get this, Darren?'

Darren shrugged. 'Found it, didn't I, Mick?'

His brother shrugged and shuffled his feet in the grass.

'No, you didn't,' Chris said angrily. 'You stole it from Brin's. What else did you steal, Darren?'

He turned to Brin but she was crouched down in the ditch. She looked up at him with joy and relief in her eyes. She stood up. 'He pinched my brother's space station . . . '

'Space station, my ass,' Darren interrupted, curling his lip in disbelief.

'Yes, space station,' Brin insisted. 'You pinched it then hid it in the hedge. My dad thought he heard someone prowling around the house during the night. I suppose you scarpered when he came out. I think we'd better get the police, Chris, don't you?'

'I didn't steal it,' Darren protested. 'I was just looking in that boathouse. Thought you'd chucked it away.'

'What rubbish,' Brin said disgustedly.

'You'd better scarper, Darren,' Chris said. 'Or we jolly well will get the police and you'll be had up for trespassing and theft.'

'Come on, Dar,' his brother said. 'Let's get out of here. They can't prove anything.'

The two brothers climbed into the car. Turning to scowl at Chris, Darren drove off, tyres spinning.

Chris crouched down. 'Is it damaged?' His voice was shaking.

Brin looked at him with shining eyes. 'No . . . it's fine. I could kill that Darren Smart,' she added angrily. 'Slob!'

'How did he know where it was?'

'I guess he must have been spying on us .. . your mum saw a car in the lane, remember? Oh, Chris, I don't care anyway. All I care is that Shannah isn't dead after all.'

'I suppose we should thank Darren, really.'

'Thank him . . . ?'

'Yes, if he hadn't pinched the egg then Shannah would really have been burned to death, wouldn't she?'

'Yes, I suppose you're right. I still think he's a slob though.'

Chris grinned. Then he said seriously, 'Brin, we've got to get her away from here. Now . . . as quickly as we can.

116

Darren knows damn well it isn't any kid's toy and I've got a horrible feeling he's determined to find out what it really is, even if it kills him!'

14

Chris—Wicken Fen

It was an ice-grey fenland morning when Chris rowed his boat the two miles to Burwell Lock. The kind of morning when all that was visible seemed to shimmer on the edge of reality. The sun, its rays dimmed by the mist, looked like a porthole in the sky. Only the distinctive 'kowk—kowk' of a startled coot broke the eerie silence. As the oars dipped through the water, Chris looked upward. It would be great if the Snowbird came out of the mist to fly over his head with her silent beating of wings. He would have liked to have seen her just once more. He felt filled with excitement and trepidation. Supposing something went wrong? Supposing they couldn't save Shannah after all? It had been bad enough after the fire—thinking the Snowbird was lost for ever. He didn't know what Brin would do if anything like that happened again. It was strange, he thought, how quickly he'd got used to having the Collins family living nearby. He remembered dreading them moving in. He must have been mad.

At dead on nine o'clock the lock keeper came out from her house.

'Mornin', Chris,' she called. 'You're up early.'

'Yep,' he said. 'Boat's been laid up for the winter, thought I'd try her out.'

Through the lock, Chris shipped the oars. He moored up past the line of motor cruisers. He made sure the tarpaulin was tucked well under the seat then began the long walk back.

At eight o'clock in the evening Brin phoned to say her parents had gone out for a meal at The Maid's Head pub in Wicken. They expected to be home about eleven.

'Chris, I'm so excited,' she whispered. 'Do you think Shannah knows it's tonight?'

Chris had the feeling she probably did. Ever since they had found the egg in the hedge and lugged it back to hide it behind the mill-tower there seemed to be a feeling of urgency in the air.

Chris set his alarm for 1 a.m. He didn't really know why he'd bothered. Even though he'd watched *L.A. Law* until 10.30, then messed around making a cup of cocoa, he still hadn't slept. He just lay under the duvet, fully clothed, waiting for his father to come up to bed. He *would* choose tonight of all nights to watch the late movie. At a quarter past midnight, Chris heard his father come upstairs. He'd been so nervous his palms were sweating. Supposing his father was still awake at 1 o'clock? What if someone saw them? Supposing a police car came along and wanted to know what they were up to?

Chris waited ten minutes, then got up quickly. He opened his bedroom door. Listened. The sound of his father's snores rumbled along the landing. Chris tip-toed to his parents' door. He listened again, holding his breath. How his mother slept through that racket he'd never know.

Downstairs, he threatened Wag with death if he made a noise. He shut the back door quietly and tip-toed round to the rear of the workshop. The old pram was covered by a sheet of polythene. Chris stuffed it behind the wheelbarrow. He pushed the pram quickly down the drive, through the gate and along the lane towards Dimmocks.

Brin was waiting. She had a blanket in her arms.

'Are they asleep?' Chris whispered.

'Yep,' Brin whispered back. 'Yours?'

'My dad stayed up to watch the movie. I nearly died.'

'Typical!'

Round the back of the mill-tower, the egg was covered with sacks. Carefully, they picked it up between them. Chris didn't remember it being so heavy. He was annoyed to find his hands were shaking.

'I hope it goes on all right,' Brin whispered.

'It should do, I measured.'

Winnie's old pram waited. Carefully, with aching arms, they laid the egg on the top. The pram wobbled and started to move away.

'The brake! The brake!' Brin hissed.

'Sorry.' Chris snapped it on with his foot.

Warily they balanced the egg, not daring to let it go until they were sure.

'It's OK,' Chris said with a confidence he didn't feel.

They covered it with the blanket, tucking it all round.

Brin giggled. Chris thought she sounded a bit hysterical. In fact he felt a bit hysterical himself.

'It looks like a giant baby.'

'Shut-up, Brin,' he hissed. 'Come on, let's get going.'

Together, they wheeled the pram around. As they did so, Chris heard Brin draw in her breath.

'Oh no . . . !' she whispered angrily. 'That's blown it.'

In the light from Brin's torch, he saw Toni standing. Watching . . .

Toni rubbed her eyes sleepily. 'What you lot up to?' she asked. She took a step forward. 'What's that?'

Brin and Chris exchanged glances.

'Nothing, Toni,' Brin said quickly. 'Go back to bed, you'll catch your death. Haven't you learned your lesson . . . ?'

But Toni came right up close. 'What's under there?'

Chris racked his brains for something to say. 'Actually, Toni,' he took Toni's arm and led her away, 'I'm really glad you're here . . . '

'Chris . . . ?' Brin began. Chris threw her a warning glance.

'Look,' he said, 'we can't explain now but we really need your help.'

'What for?' Toni asked suspiciously. She shivered. She pulled the edges of her dressing gown together.

'Well, how do you fancy a bike ride?'

'What, in the dark?' Toni said, her voice full of doubt.

'Yes,' Chris said. 'We're taking this . . . this . . . ' he indicated the pram, '. . . to . . . well, you'll see when we get there. If you ride in front on your mountain bike you can show us the way with your lamp.'

'The way to where . . . ?' Toni looked even more dubious.

'If she doesn't want to . . .' Brin began.

'I do, I do,' Toni said. 'But why are you taking that stupid old pr—?'

'We'll explain later. Now, you sure you want to help us?'

'Yes.' Toni nodded vehemently.

'OK. Go and get your coat and boots.'

Toni came back with her coat and helmet on. 'I still want to know what's in the pram.'

'You'll find out later,' Brin interrupted. Then she put her hand on Toni's shoulder. 'Toni, you've got to be quiet or we'll get found out.'

'Come on, you lot,' Chris said impatiently. 'We haven't got all night.'

Half-way along the lane they heard a car coming.

'Quick,' Brin said. Her voice sounded on the edge of panic.

Chris hoped it wasn't Darren Smart again. He wouldn't put it past him.

'Toni . . . ' Brin called urgently. 'Switch off your lamp.'

They dived on to the verge, the pram bumping over the slushy ground. Water and mud splashed over their legs. They ducked down behind a willow tree. A branch scratched Chris's face.

A car sped past, the wide beam of its lights sweeping the road.

They breathed a sigh of relief.

When they reached the lock-keeper's house, the gate was padlocked.

'Now what do we do?' Brin said anxiously.

'We passed a gate,' Toni piped up. 'Just down there. It was half open.'

'You sure?' Brin had been too intent on keeping the pram steady to notice.

''Course I'm sure.'

'Come on then.'

They ran back along the road, Toni pedalling ahead.

'Here,' she called.

Chris sighed. 'She'd wake the dead your sister.'

'You're telling me?'

But Toni was right. The field gate was ajar. She pushed it fully open with her front wheel. The others came through.

Keeping close to the fence they pushed the pram along the field edge. Once or twice it got stuck, bogged down in the waterlogged, black soil. Toni got off her bike to help them pull it out. Eventually, they managed to haul the pram up, over the steep bank, to the river. In the lock-keeper's house a dog barked.

'Ssh!' Brin hissed although none of them were making a sound. They crouched down, holding their breath.

'Come on,' Chris whispered. 'The boat's just along here.'

Chris slid down the bank. He took the tarpaulin from under the seat. 'Let's get her in.'

'Who's her?' Toni asked.

Brin sighed. 'Shut-up, Toni, will you?' She uncovered the egg.

Chris heard Toni whistle. 'What is THAT?' she said.

'I'll tell you on the way, OK?' Chris said.

Together they half rolled the egg, half pushed it down the steep slope, into the boat. Chris gently eased it into the bottom. He took the tarpaulin from under the seat and covered it up.

'Leave your bike by that motor cruiser,' Brin said to Toni. 'We'll pick it up on the way back.'

Chris held out his hand. 'Hurry up, for goodness' sake!' When they were sitting down, he said, 'OK, you lot, let's go.'

'Where?' Toni asked.

'To Wicken Fen.'

'What for?'

'You'll see,' Brin said.

* * *

They rowed along in silence. The only sound was the soft splish of oars in the water, the occasional, startled, 'pip, pip' of a disturbed bird. Brin sat with Toni in the bow. One hand steadied the egg, the other held the torch.

'Tell me then,' Toni said suddenly, breaking the spell of silence. 'I want to know.'

In a soft voice, Chris told her the story of Shannah. Once or twice Toni gasped, her eyes wide with disbelief. When he mentioned the fire, she began to cry.

Brin put her arm round her sister's shoulder. 'Don't cry, Toni . . . you weren't to know.'

'You should have told me,' Toni sobbed. 'I wouldn't have said anything.'

'You must promise now never, ever to tell anyone,' Chris said gently.

Toni shook her head. 'I won't. I promise.'

Chris looked up to see Brin raise her eyebrows and smile at him.

After that they rowed in silence again. They reached the bridge and branched off left into Wicken Lode.

'What if it doesn't come?' Brin said. She shivered. A breeze had sprung up. It whispered through the trees like voices.

'It will,' Chris pulled heavily on the oars. 'I know it will. It's been here all winter, even when food was scarce. I know it will come.'

'I wish we could wait for it.'

Chris shook his head. 'It could be ages. They probably won't go off for a week or two, even longer. It depends on the weather.'

'I hope she'll be all right.'

'It's a chance we've got to take,' Chris said grimly.

'How much further?' Toni said impatiently.

'Nearly there.'

They came to a place where the lode narrowed. Chris manoeuvred the boat towards the sedge-covered marshland on the opposite side to the bank.

'We've just got to go into the reed beds,' he explained to Toni.

'Here . . . ' Brin handed her the torch. 'Shine it for us, will you?'

Using one oar as a paddle Chris propelled the boat as far as it would go into the reeds.

'Won't it go any further?' Brin asked anxiously.

He shook his head. 'No. We'll have to leave her here.'

'Will she be hidden enough?'

'She'll have to be.'

Chris shook off the tarpaulin and folded it in two. He leaned out as far as he dared and laid it on a bed of reeds. Together, carefully, he and Brin lifted the silver-grey egg from the bottom of the boat. Kneeling, they leaned precariously over the gunwale. Brin almost lost her balance. Toni grasped the back of her coat, hanging on for dear life. Banging her elbows painfully, she just managed to save herself before the egg fell out of her grasp. Panting, they laid the egg to rest gently on the tarpaulin.

'Whew!' Brin said. 'Thought I was a goner then.' She rubbed her elbow ruefully.

'I want to see her,' Toni said, matter-of-factly.

Brin looked at Chris. 'I want to see her, too, just one more time.'

'Me too,' Chris said.

Brin fumbled in her pocket. She drew out a piece of paper. 'I copied out the key,' she said. 'I hope it's right.'

'Oh . . . it's Tom's dream,' said Toni, her voice filled with amazement. She leaned forward to get a better look.

'Yes.' Chris shone the torch while Brin punched in the code.

Toni began to tap her feet impatiently.

'Sit still . . . please, Toni,' Chris said.

Just then the clouds parted and the half-moon came out. Suddenly, it was almost as bright as day. As it did so, the egg began to hum and sing. The dark line appeared round its middle and the lid slowly began to open.

Instead of stopping half-way, this time it opened fully. Inside lay Shannah. Still asleep. Still warm.

'Oh!' Toni gave a little cry. 'Isn't she pretty.'

Brin put her arm across Toni's shoulders. 'Yes,' she said, her voice sounding crackly. 'Isn't she.' Above Toni's head Chris looked at her and smiled.

'Can I touch her?' Toni's face was red and eager in the moonlight.

'Very gently.'

She held the back of Toni's coat as she leaned out and touched the satin feathers.

'She feels like silk,' she whispered. 'Why has she got that crest on her head?'

'It's just the way she's made.'

'She's not like E.T. or anything.'

'No.' Brin smiled. 'She's not a bit like E.T. But I think she's probably just as nice.'

Toni leaned out further.

'Careful, Toni!' The last thing they needed was for Toni to go tumbling over the side.

'There's something under her wing.'

Toni's chubby hand disappeared beneath the feathers. When she withdrew it, there was an object dangling from her fingers.

She struggled backwards into the boat.

'Look,' she said.

Moonlight reflected gold.

'What is it?' Chris asked.

Brin took it from Toni. She looked at Chris in wonder. Then at Toni.

'It's mine,' Toni said. She made a grab for it. 'I found it . . . !'

'Just a minute!' Brin held it up by its golden chain. It swung in front of their eyes hypnotically. 'It's Winnie's locket,' Brin whispered. 'I know it is.'

'That means . . . ' Chris said.

'Yes . . . ' she answered. 'It means she did find Shannah after all.'

Brin put the piece of precious jewellery in her pocket.

'Hey . . . ' Toni protested.

'I'll look after it for now, Toni.'

'It's not fair . . . '

As Toni spoke, the egg began to close.

'Have we got to leave her now?' Toni asked.

'Yes,' Brin said sadly. 'I'm afraid we have.'

Chris handed Brin an oar and carefully they pushed Shannah deeper into the reeds. They seemed to part before her, then close again like a comforting hand. When they couldn't reach any further, the egg had disappeared completely. They sat in silence for a minute.

'When will the snow-goose fly away?' Toni asked softly.

'We hope it will go back with the flock of brent geese to the Arctic regions when the weather here starts to warm up.'

'How will Shannah know she's got to follow it?'

'I told her,' Brin said. 'When she was still up in the mill-tower. I hope she heard me OK. If not . . . well, maybe we'll never know.'

'Shouldn't we say a prayer or something?' Toni whispered.

Brin smiled. 'No, Toni, I don't think we need do anything like that.'

'But I'm sure she's an angel.'

Brin looked at Chris but he was staring into space.

'Come on,' she whispered. 'Let's go home.'

15

Brin—The Flight of the Snow-goose

By the end of the week the snow had totally gone. The bitter, Fenland winter Brin thought would never end, seemed as if it had happened a hundred years ago. As soon as there was a hint of spring, the land became a hive of activity.

One morning during half term Brin came back from shopping in Cambridge with Alex to find Chris sitting at the kitchen table. He had come to ask if Brin wanted to walk along the river, try to see the heron he had been telling her about. She had spoken to him several times on the phone to ask if he had seen any geese, flying north.

'No,' he had said sadly. 'I've got a horrible feeling we may have been too late.'

Toni and Tom were sitting with Chris and their father, munching biscuits. Toni kept smiling secretively, first at Chris, then at Brin as she sat beside him, her hands round a mug of hot coffee. Alex had gone back out to have a word with Mr Gibbs in the mill-tower.

Brin could see Chris was trying to ignore Toni's secret glances.

'Have you told Chris about these?' David said. He picked up a pile of old documents and papers.

'No,' Brin said. 'Not yet.'

'What are they?' Chris asked.

'Documents the solicitor sent. Stuff belonging to my aunt.'

'Oh.'

'They've solved quite a few mysteries. That and finding Winnie's locket. Bit of luck that, eh?'

'Yes,' Chris said. Out of the corner of his eye he saw Toni smile then cover her face with her hands.

'Trust Toni,' David said. 'Taking the back off that old clock to see how it worked. Going to be an engineer that girl.'

'What a place to hide a locket,' Toni said, giggling.

Brin had a horrible, sinking feeling she was going to give the game away any minute.

'Go and get the locket, Toni,' David said. 'I'm sure Chris would like to see it.'

Toni came back with a leather box. She opened it carefully. Lying on cotton wool was the gold locket.

'Open it, then,' David urged.

Inside the locket were two brown and faded miniature photographs. A man and a woman. Stern looking. Dressed in strange clothes.

Chris looked closer. 'That's not Mrs Mirston is it?'

'We think it must have been Uncle Jacob's parents.' David pointed. 'Alex thinks they're dressed in Polish national costume.'

'Polish . . .?'

'Yes. I'm surprised Brin hasn't told you . . .'

'I was going to,' Brin interrupted. 'I just haven't had the chance yet.'

'Anyway,' David continued, '. . . we've discovered from the documents that Uncle Jacob was Polish. We think he was probably a prisoner of war.'

'Oh . . .?'

'Yes. During the First World War prisoners were sent over here to work on farms . . . and apparently Winnie lived on a farm in Wales. We think Jacob was sent to work there . . .'

'And that's how Winnie . . . er, I mean Mrs Mirston, met him?'

'Right.'

'Do you think that's why her family disapproved—because he was a prisoner of war?'

'No doubt about it. You see she was very young, and the family were quite wealthy. I expect they had someone else in mind for her. Probably another landowner. They did that in those days.'

'What?'

'Marry their children off to other landowners. That's how they got really rich, you see.'

'Oh,' Chris said.

'Good idea if you ask me.' David grinned.

Brin snorted and punched her father's arm. 'You don't mean that, Dad,' she said.

'We thought they didn't like him because being an artist wasn't respectable,' Chris said.

'Yes, we thought that too. But I suspect that was just one of many reasons. Not the least that he was a foreigner.'

'Can't see what difference that makes.'

'Well, people were a bit paranoid about strangers in those days. They didn't travel like we do now and they couldn't understand the ways of people from other countries. To them, it would have been almost as if Uncle Jacob came from another planet.'

'It would be like us hating . . .' Toni hesitated.

'Hating who, Toni?' her father asked.

'Oh, er . . .' Toni said. She glanced at Brin who gave her the fiercest frown she could muster. 'No one . . .' She closed the locket and put it into its box. 'Brin's going to have it when she's older,' she said, pushing out her bottom lip. 'Even though *I* found it.'

'Toni, we have explained . . .' her father began.

'I know, I know. She's the oldest, blah, blah, blah . . .'

Chris grinned.

'I'll let you borrow it,' Brin said. '*If* you're good.'

Toni stuck her tongue out. 'Have you let that swan go yet, Chris?' she asked.

'Yes, er . . . on Wednesday.'

'Was it OK?'

'Fine.'

'You're good at rescuing things, aren't you?' she said knowingly.

Brin dreaded what she might say next.

'Am I?' Chris said, glancing at Brin. 'I don't really know.'

* * *

'Have you seen anything?' Brin asked later when they were alone.

Chris shook his head. 'No. I've been hoping to go out to Wicken but I haven't had a chance. It's been so mild, I've really got a feeling we were too late. But I've been keeping an eye out.'

Brin looked sad. 'Me too. I did want to see her go, didn't you?'

'Yes,' Chris said.

'Maybe we could go out there together . . . today . . . now!'

'OK,' Chris said. 'I wanted to go for a walk anyway.'

'Great. I'll just go and get my boots.'

'Do you think Toni'll lend you her bike, otherwise we'll be all day?'

'Dunno, I'll ask.'

'No,' Toni said.

'Oh, Ant . . .!'

'Sit on my crossbar if you like, then,' Chris volunteered.

'OK.' Brin stuck her tongue out at her sister.

Along the river Brin told Chris more about her great-great-aunt.

'. . . and Uncle Jacob's real name was Mirski,' she said. 'He changed it to Mirston. Lots of foreigners changed their names when they came to live in England after the war apparently.'

'You know . . .' Chris was thinking of what Brin's father had said. 'It's funny how people were so paranoid about foreigners . . . still are, some of them.'

'Yes,' Brin said thoughtfully. 'And that's why we *had* to rescue Shannah. And why we must never, ever, tell anybody else. It must always be our secret Chris, ours and Toni's.'

Chris nodded in agreement.

'I'm so glad we found the locket,' Brin said. 'And Toni really did put it inside the case of that old clock, so it wasn't really a fib, was it?'

Chris looked at her. He grinned. 'No,' he said, 'not *really*.'

'Do you think that's what she was doing?'

'Who . . .? When . . .?'

'Aunt Winnie, when your mum found her at the bottom of the stairs. Do you think she had just given the locket to Shannah?'

'She could have. Mum said she was sure Mrs Mirston was wearing it the day before.'

'Anyway,' Brin said. 'At least we've solved the mystery of Uncle Jacob. You know . . . I really feel sorry for them.'

'Why?'

'Well, being cut off from their family and all that.'

'Mum said Winnie loved the Fens. She said that although the old girl could hardly remember what happened yesterday her memories of years ago were as clear as anything. And she was always happy. She'd said to Mum that all they ever wanted to do was be together.'

Brin sighed. 'It's ever so romantic.'

Chris made a noise that sounded like a snort.

Brin looked at him. 'Well . . . it is. Just the two of them . . .'

'And Shannah,' Chris said.

'Yes . . . and Shannah.' Brin's voice sounded sad. Chris glanced at her quickly. Her eyes were bright with moisture. 'Oh, Chris . . .' she said. 'I wish we could see her just once more.'

'You never know,' he said unconvincingly. 'Maybe we will.'

'No.' Brin shook her head. 'I don't think so somehow.'

There were great flocks of wild fowl out at Wicken Fen. But the snow-goose wasn't amongst them.

'They're still here,' Brin said, pointing to a flock of big, black-necked geese alighting on the marshlands. 'So maybe the snow-goose is too.'

'No, they're Canada geese, they live here all the year.' Chris pointed. 'See those . . .' Another flock were coming in to land, honking and trumpeting like a carnival. '*They're* the dark-breasted brents we saw the snow-goose with.'

'Where do they breed?'

'On the shores and islands of the Arctic, north eastern Siberia, places like that.'

'So if the snow-goose sticks with them and Shannah follows it . . .'

'That's right,' Chris said. 'All she'll have to do is keep flying north until she reaches the polar regions . . .'

'Where she'll find a winterland, a landscape that's like her home planet.'

'Hope so,' Chris said.

'So if the snow-goose doesn't come, Shannah will still be . . . ?' Brin didn't want to think about it any more.

Chris glanced at his watch. 'I've got to get back, Brin, I promised to help my dad.'

'What if the snow-goose doesn't come, Chris?' Brin's eyes were threatening to spill over.

Chris shrugged. He glanced at Brin then looked away. 'I dunno,' he said gruffly.

'We could take her back home again,' Brin suggested. 'Keep her until next year.'

'No. She won't survive. It's now or never.'

Brin thought her parents must have decided she'd turned over a new leaf. She spent so much time in her room, supposedly doing her homework, they probably thought the country air was working miracles. Most of the time, though, she was gazing out of her bedroom window. Hoping to see the flight of the snow-goose, heading for home. She knew Chris had been right when he said it was now . . . or never.

After a week or so she had almost given up. In fact she and Chris didn't even talk about it any more. Chris went back to Wicken a couple of times. Once with Ben Smith to bird-watch. Once on his own in his boat when he should have been at school. He phoned Brin later to say most of the winter visitors had already gone home. His voice was full of regret.

* * *

One weekend, Alex and David took the Collins children to see the Stretham Pump Engine. They stopped at Highfen for eggs on the way home. Mrs Carter asked them in.

'Chris is outside somewhere if you want to see him,' she said to Brin.

'I'll come,' Toni said. 'I want to show him this plan of how the Engine works.'

'I expect he's seen it hundreds of times.'

'I bet he hasn't.'

They crossed the yard.

Mr Carter was hosing down one of the tractors.

'Hello, you two, looking for Christopher? He's taken the dog along the river. Only just gone, if you hurry you'll catch him up.'

Brin didn't feel much like hurrying. Toni ran on ahead.

'Be careful,' Brin called. The last thing she felt like having to do was dive in the river to rescue Toni from drowning.

'I will,' Toni called, skipping along.

Brin dawdled along the bank. In the shallows, a herd of black and white cows had come down to the water to drink. They lifted their heads as Toni skipped by. By a clump of willows Brin saw her stop suddenly, then she disappeared. Brin quickened her step, expecting to hear a splash. When none came she slowed down again, kicking at the grass as she walked. Above, the muddy March sky was streaked with silver. As Brin looked skyward, a formation of geese flew high, etched black against the silver-grey clouds. Brin wondered what species they were. If they were headed for the warmer, western shores of North America or if they were the ones she'd been looking for. The dark-breasted geese that would be heading for arctic Europe, the snow-goose in their wake. They flew so high there was no way of telling.

When Brin reached the willows she saw the reason for Toni's sudden disappearance. Chris was sitting on a tree root at the water's edge. He had an arm round Toni's shoulders. The other was holding Wag's collar. Tight. They were all sitting very still. For a change Toni wasn't nattering nineteen to the dozen. Then Brin saw why. On the opposite bank stood a stately grey heron. Its neck was outstretched, one leg tucked up.

She sat down beside Chris and Toni. The only sound was the lapping of water against the bank. Chris grinned at her and held his finger to his lips.

Wag wagged his tail.

The heron looked at them. Then, without warning, it spread its great wings and took off. Slowly, majestically, it flew low over the Fen. Then, gaining height it gradually disappeared. Its grey coat blended with the sky as if it was made of the same material.

'Wow!' Toni said.

'Sorry if I frightened it off,' Brin said.

'You didn't.' Chris stood up. 'I'd been watching it ages anyway.'

They began to walk back along the bank. The dog ran on ahead. Brin bent to pick up a stick to throw for him.

'This is the place we first saw . . .' she began sadly. As she spoke, Toni suddenly pointed upwards.

'Look you two,' she said in quite an ordinary voice. It was as if the most utterly brilliant thing in their whole lives wasn't just about to happen. 'What kind of bird is THAT?'

And there, way above their heads, flew the snow-goose. Its mellow, bell-like voice echoed across the sky like a signal. They stood motionless, staring up at the sky as if they had been turned into statues. Brin held her breath.

And then they saw something they had hoped and dreamed of for weeks. For behind the snow-goose, on wings the colour of moonlight, flew the figure of Shannah. Even at that distance they could see her huge wingspan, following the snow-goose like a great shadow in the sky. As they watched, spellbound, Shannah broke away. She circled. Lower and lower towards them. Gradually her voice came through the silence. Not the sad-song Brin and Chris remembered but a new sound, high pitched and joyous. She circled once more, her great wing-beating making no sound. Then she soared away in the wake of the snow-goose and was gone from the Fenland for ever.

After a minute of breathless silence Toni said in a funny, squeaky voice. 'Wow! Was that . . .?'

'Yes,' Chris and Brin said together, smiling. 'It was.'

Then they hugged each other and leapt and danced and whooped as if they were a great flock of geese themselves. Chris grabbed Toni's football scarf and ran along the bank waving it like a flag of triumph. He ran around in a circle shouting like a maniac. Wag jumped round him, barking. Then Chris fell down in the grass and rolled over and over, still yelling. It was the loudest noise Brin had ever heard him make. The dog leapt on top of him and began licking his face.

'He's nutty,' Toni said. Then shouted too when Brin hugged her so tightly she could hardly breathe.

Brin knew she would never forget that evening. The three of them walking home, arms round each other, laughing and talking as if a great weight had been lifted from their shoulders. And getting back to Highfen. Sitting round the fire drinking cups of hot chocolate. All the grown-ups asking what had happened to make them look so happy. They didn't tell them of course. They just said they'd been mucking about. What could they have said anyway?

Who would ever have believed the tale of their fabulous Snowbird winter?

Going home in the car, Alex put her favourite tape in the machine.

'Oh, no,' Tom groaned, pulling his green baseball cap over his eyes. 'Not the Beatles. Not "When I'm Sixty-four"!'

But they had heard it so often they all sang along anyway.

END

The excerpt from "Elizabeth Woodcock's Dreadful Experience" on p 93 is taken from *Tales of Old Cambridgeshire* by Polly Howat published by Countryside Books, 3, Catherine Road, Newbury, Berks.

The newspaper report of Elizabeth's tragedy is in the *Cambridgeshire Independent Press and Chronicle*, 16 February 1799.